A Glass of Two Milks

If I have the gift of prophecy, and know all mysteries and all knowledge; and if I have all faith, so as to remove mountains, but do not have love, I am nothing.
1 Corinthians 13

© Nigel Lesmoir-Gordon
2016

Published by Gordon Books

April Cottage, Clophill, Bedfordshire MK45 4AD

Copyright © 2016 by Nigel Lesmoir-Gordon

ISBN
Paperback: 978-0-9573067-8-3
E-book: 978-0-9573067-9-0

This story is set in 2030. It continues the gripping, roller-coaster saga of writer John Smith, mathematician Susie Bellavista and battle-hardened Biro as once again they have to wage war with Tigran Gevorkian, diving right into the eye of the storm as they take on the New World Order Movement. 2030 is a high-tech utopian world, but one that is still subject to all the usual human failings - lust, anger, greed, attachment and egotism. Will the team succeed? Be prepared for some surprises.

SOME REVIEWS

A zippy number. The characters are sharp and intriguing. Great dialogue with a plot that moves along. I like the 'soft' futuristic setting. It's a world mostly like ours but with extra and intriguing layers.
Andrew Rawlinson. Author.

Nigel's imagination is fantastic! The world he creates is not saved by a conventional Messiah... I like the way that the author speaks directly to the reader.
Sarah Chatwin. Author.

This book is a page tuner. It's gripping and mind expanding. I love its pace and style. The writer is detached from the story and yet right in it. Marie-Michel Bailey. Art Critic.

A Glass of Two Milks is beautifully written. The author has a first rate command of the English language and his literary style makes this book a treat to read. Mary Thomas. Teacher.

Nigel Lesmoir-Gordon is a visionary and an entertainer. He writes a gripping tale with confidence, humour and flair.
Harvey Brownwood-Fox. Entrepreneur.

A Glass of Two Milks is dedicated to:
My wife Jenny for being herself.
Bella our dog for barking and holding the fort.
Chris Case, who one crazy night in '65 uttered the
profound and timeless phrase which has now become
the title of this book.

Cover design by Gabriel Lesmoir-Gordon.

Chapter One
The Car

I needed a drink, I needed a lot of life insurance, I needed a vacation, I needed a home in the country. What I had was a coat, a hat and a gun. I put them on and went out of the room.
Raymond Chandler in *Farewell, My Lovely*

It all kicked off with the Hispano Suiza. It was a cream and brown '35 Convertible - an enormous, elegant, and eye-catching limousine. Biro was still driving it and, although somewhat ostentatious, it suited John and Biro well. They were close friends and partners in a film production company with Hollywood connections, producing successful, mid-budget feature films. Biro had taken the Hispano from Tigran Gevorkian in lieu of unpaid wages and expenses and in settlement for all the grief he caused them when he stole John's computer with the only copy of his latest novel on its hard-drive. Gevorkian could have found them but made no effort until he saw them in the Hispano outside Fortnum and Mason one balmy spring morning. Seeing it again stung like lemon juice poured on an open wound.

Thing was, Gevorkian had wanted to get the Hispano Suiza back and had made a huge effort to find John and Susie. He wanted Biro too. Of course, he couldn't report the loss of the car. He couldn't go near the cops. But, as they now realised, he never gave up.

They found out later that he had tracked them down in Cambridge and set a surveillance team onto them. As Bob Dylan sang in *Hurricane* "...*They had no idea what kinda shit was about to go down.*"

John's beautiful wife Susie was a fellow at Trinity College and was heading-up the university's Department of Pure Mathematics. She had an outstanding mind and was blessed too with classic good looks. She had the finest features, brown eyes and blonde hair that hung in waves to below her shoulders. She had the body of an athlete, slim, but beautifully proportioned, delicate and classically feminine. She carried herself with confidence and never failed to turn the heads of both men and women on the street. She had charisma, powerful intelligence and natural confidence. She had achieved recognition for her work on quantum computing algorithms and quantum information theory where mathematics met physics. It was highly significant work with huge potential and it had led to enormous progress in the field of quantum computing.

Both John and Susie travelled a lot: Susie lecturing and John filming in various corners of the world but they had remained very close and loyal. She was the love of John's life and he was sure that it would always be this way. In his industry he met a lot of beautiful women but his head had never been seriously turned and he was rarely tempted into another woman's bed.

John was a tall, good looking, muscular man with hands at once strong and delicate. He was posh and public school through and through, but he was no snob. He had come out of the creative doldrums when his first novel *Clusterfuck* had been picked up by a major Hollywood studio and turned into a blockbuster film, which was released to the world under the softer title *Green as Grass*. It earned him shed-loads of money.

They had two children. Their daughter Bella-Blue was two years older than their son Felix. The name means happy or lucky and Felix first started to show signs of being 'different' when he turned eight. This was about the time their dog Jane died. So, in a way, some bad stuff happened all at once and John found out that he did not lead as charmed a life as he had assumed he did back in 2011. Like his mother Felix had always been way ahead of his peer group at school. Again it was mathematics which made him stand out. Looking back over history it's clear that many brilliant mathematicians had also been mentally unstable and been prone to bouts of mania and depression. Par for the course. So when Felix exhibited signs of mania at the age of 12 they were very frightened but not all that surprised. Susie had told John way back there was a strain of bipolar affective disorder running through her family line. Her uncle, March Klossowski, who had helped years earlier on a project of John's, was bipolar. When John met him he hadn't had an episode in over 30 years but there were others in her family on Susie's mother's side, who had suffered with this terrifying and mysterious affliction. Felix experienced his first full-blown manic episode in the following year. Bella-Blue, was thankfully as level as the Cambridge fens. She was working in Sydney and missed all of the forthcoming action.

Susie had been an outstanding maths student from a very early age, a prodigy. She passed college entrance exams when she was just fifteen. She went first to Yale and then on to Cambridge. When John met her she was already a professor at UCL and she was only twenty-five.

They had been living in Cambridge for several years when Felix's first manic episode struck. They moved there for the schools and the extra tuition Felix required to guide him through the impenetrable morass of mathematics. There were still many unsolved problems in this field and new discoveries were waiting to be made even though so much in the world had changed since Susie and John first met.

Chapter Two
Felix

None are more hopelessly enslaved than those who falsely believe they are free.

Johann Wolfgang von Goethe

Biro and John were working on a big film project which involved a lot of travelling in their search for locations when Felix disappeared. He walked to school one morning and didn't return in the evening. No one at the school could throw any light on what might have happened to him. Susie and John spoke to all his friends and combed the area around their house but there was no sign of him. After a feeble attempt to do his morning meditation John called the police and they instigated a search. Susie was beside herself. John couldn't calm her and he wasn't in such a good state himself. One of them had to hold things together and that for a change was John. He found Felix's locator on his desk. Not very helpful of him. John tried StarScan without success. No surprises there. Neither of them could sleep that first night. Susie sat up with her weblink in her lap and John walked the streets.

The sun rose into a bright but hazy sky and John made his way home, empty-handed. He felt lost and very sad. He thought about the death of their dog Jane. She died just three months ago and they all missed her. Thinking of that beautiful little Jack Russell broke his heart all over again. He walked into a small copse, sat against a tree and wept great choking sobs.

John was sitting alone in the kitchen later trying to pull himself together, staring at a bowl of breakfast cereal when Baby Cakes, their production manager, arrived. He let himself in and called from the hall.

'You there, John?'

'In the kitchen.'

Baby Cakes stood in the doorway, looking at him. 'You OK, Boss?'

He took a few seconds to gather himself before he answered. 'No, I'm not.'

'Why, what's up?'

'Felix didn't come home last night.'

'He'll be OK and home soon.' Baby Cakes joined John at the table. 'But I had this strange dream.'

'How d'you mean?'

'I…well, don't really know…it's just that…'

'Yes?'

''Bout Felix…'

'And?'

'I saw him.'

'You...saw him?'

Baby Cakes sighed and looked away. 'I...he was in a white room...looked like a basement...no windows.'

'What was he...?

'He was tied to a chair. It looked painful. But...I saw no injuries.'

John stood up and walked round the table to stand next to Baby Cakes. 'Where was this room, Cakes?'

'I dunno...could be anywhere...just a room.'

'Nothing you recognised?'

'No.'

John walked to the window and looked out over the sunlit garden.

'It was just a dream, Boss. Might not mean anything.'

John turned back to him. 'But it... fits.'

Susie walked into the hall and called out. 'Who is it, John?'

'Baby Cakes.'

'Has he...?'

'No...just come round for work.'

Susie went back to the sitting-room.

'How is she?'

John was irritated. 'How d' you think?'

'Sorry, Boss.'

They stood in silence looking out of the window.

'D'you want something, Boss?'

'Mean get stoned?'

'No something…to lift you up.'

'No thanks, Cakes. I just… that I… don't know what to do. Got to find Felix.'

'Of course…but maybe he'll walk in here any minute.'

John's weblink chimed. He jumped and opened the line. He listened then mouthed to Baby Cakes, 'It's the cops.'

John listened, then, 'Nothing…what's your next move?' 'Do your best…thanks…I'll wait here.' He closed the connection and walked to the kitchen door. 'Wait here. Oh, and call Biro please. I'm gonna talk to Susie. Won't be long.'

'Shall I ask him to come back here?'

'No let him finish what he's doing. Not a lot he can do here. Tell him I'll see him later this morning.' John left the room.

Baby Cakes took his handle from John's first novel *Clusterfuck*. It was the name of one of the stoned-out grunts in a platoon which gets cut off behind enemy lines eventually making it to the coast and freedom. Only his friends could address him like this. To others he was addressed as Kirk or as Mr Semple by lower echelon crew members.

Biro was just back from Afghanistan with a small unit setting up locations doing some preliminary casting for a film they were making on the futile efforts of the Coalition forces to suppress The Taliban back in the early 2000s. Many, many lives had been thrown away there. You would've have thought that the invading forces might have learnt the lesson that Afghanistan was an impossible place to fight in and control. The Brits had tried it and the Soviets had tried it and failed. Do people never learn? Their film was to be about the freedom fighters who eventually kicked out the Coalition. They never did get that oil pipe line through there and anyway it wasn't needed now as oil has had its day. The only half-way decent thing to come out of that conflict was the BBC comedy series *Bluestone 42* back in 2013. It must've been good because John still talked about it and remembered some of the lines.

John walked into the sitting-room. Susie lay scrunched up on the long sofa under the bay window. Dappled sunlight played over her. She was as beautiful as ever. She raised her head to glance at John. She looked exhausted, drained. Dark rings framed her brown eyes. She attempted a smile then started to sob. John walked over to her and held her in his arms. He loved her more with each passing day and he needed her now so much just as she needed him.

'What're we goin' to do, John?'

'I don't know, darling. Maybe he'll just come home.'

'Yes but he isn't… well.'

'I know. I know.'

'So?'

'So maybe he'll do something… wild and get picked up by the cops.'

Susie shuddered and buried her head in the cushions. John watched her silently, lost for words.

Baby Cakes called from the kitchen, 'I'm going up to the office, Boss. Got some things to do.'

'OK, Cakes. I'll see you up there in a while.' John stood, touched Susie on the shoulder and walked out of the room but he didn't join Baby Cakes. He left the house and walked down towards the river, scanning to the left and right for any sign of Felix. He was always drawn to the river and often hung-out there. John wound his way down to the water, sat on the bank and stared into the slow-flowing stream. He let his mind flow through Felix - his likes, dislikes, beliefs and inclinations.

Chapter Three
Docs 'n' Drones

'But who has gathered the world in his fists?
Who has bound the waters in a garment?
Thomas Hardy

We can't avoid conflict so we have to understand the nature of conflict. To attempt to escape conflict we take to drink, sex, church, organized religions, social activities, superficial amusements - every form of escape. We have tried to avoid conflict but we haven't been able to. The very avoidance contributes to conflict.

John knew that Susie was working on something important, which she wouldn't discuss with him. Reading between the lines, though, he understood it had something to do with The New World Order Movement whose said goal was the elimination of black, brown and oriental people from the surface of the planet to establish an all-white, caucasian race. Yikes! So for all the advances that had been made there was still trouble and strife. Jealousy, greed, racism, egotism and lust continued to haunt the world. But John assumed that was inevitable and just the way it goes. This thought made him go gloomy and grey and not a little depressed. He couldn't get his head round what the movement really wanted. Power? What d'you do with power when you've got it? It seemed crazy to him but then he couldn't get inside the minds of the people behind the movement. And, to be honest, he didn't want to. He left it to Susie. She seemed able to cope. He got on with making entertaining and inspiring films. Oh yes, they still had cinemas and not every film was 3D. People still liked to go out to the flicks even though they could watch films as holographs in their own homes.

John headed to his office on King's Parade. As he walked down Benet Street he called up Dr Floyd, Felix's shrink.

'Hi, Doc... Felix didn't come home last night... Yes, I've called the cops and Biro has put up some camera drones... Yeah, OK, I'll keep you informed... 'bye now.' He strode into the office projecting an air of confidence - not at all how he really felt inside.

'Morning all.' He stopped at reception. 'Anything urgent needing my attention?'

'No. Cakes has everything under control.'

'Right. Good. Ask Mary to come through to my office, please.'

He sat down at his desk and switched on the drone monitor channel. He could see that Biro had put six into the air and that they were doing an organized sweep. Following the disastrous reign of the war-mongering George W Bush and his devil sidekick Tony Blair, who together brought havoc and destruction to the Middle East, drones had reached a high level of development. The Coalition had sought a power base in the region and control of the oil. Obama fought on with armed drones. At the time of writing these remote weapons had been made illegal throughout the world. John would never forget watching teenage game-players flying drones over Afghanistan and Pakistan, launching fearsome missiles tipped with depleted uranium for increased 'effect'. And all for oil! Can you believe it? Well, it is true and it did happen. As quoted in a Wall Street journal edition at that time "Drones Make War Fighting More Humane." Holy shit!

Mary came in and sat down opposite him. She looked ill at ease.

'What's up, Mary?'

'Biro told me about Felix…that he didn't come home.'

'That's right, dear. We don't know where he is right now.'

'I'm sorry to hear that, John.'

He put on a brave face. 'I'm sure he's OK. He'll be home soon.'

'I hope so, John.' She looked down at her feet, clearly ill at ease.

'OK, Mary, let's get on with some work. Biro'll be here shortly.' And right on cue he walked into the room. He was a well-built Hungarian guy with cropped hair, handsome in a rugged, weather-beaten way and a few years older than John. He was an ex-soldier, who'd seen some combat back in the day. Hard-core with a big heart, you might say.

'Hi, John. Any news on Felix?'

'No.'

'The drones haven't clocked up anything yet. Might use the heat-seeking function.'

'Sounds like a good idea.'

'I'll set it up.' He sat down in the chair opposite John.

'So how's it going in Afghanistan?'

'Goes good, John. Found some truly outstanding locations. Real dramatic stuff. Got a few good faces lined up too. We shot some fine footage when you're ready to take a look and we set up some first class contacts in the tribes. They're on our side. So, all in all…'

The big wall screen abruptly lit up.

'Holy shit!' Biro's draw dropped.

John glanced at him and then at the screen. They saw a two-metre tall super hi-def image of Tigran Gevorkian's mug.

'Good morning, gentlemen.' He waited for a response,

which he didn't get. 'No need to be uncivil.'

'Fuck you!' was Biro's response.

'Now, now, Biro. No need to be rude.'

'What d'ya want, Gevorkian?'

A big smile spread across the Armenian's face. He had them on the back foot.

'I want my car back, Biro.'

'Fuck off.'

He continued to smile. It was disconcerting. 'I have your son.'

'What!'

'I have your son, John.'

'You kidnapped Felix to bargain for your car!'

'Not just my car. I want the algorithm your wife is working on for the Consortium.'

'How d'you know about that?' This was déjà vu. It took John back to 2011 when Gevorkian stole his computer, which held the only copy he had of his second novel Nothing and Everywhere. They got the computer back. Gevorkian had hidden a program on the PC and had to steal it because John's phone had been disconnected as a result of him not being able to pay the phone bill. There were two good sides to this story though. He met Susie and Biro.

'Felix told me.'

'How did he know about the algorithm?'

'He heard his mother talking on the phone. She should've been more careful.'

I felt my anger boiling up. 'Why'd he tell you?'

Ah hah.'

'Ah hah, what?

'It's long story.'

'We got time. Tell us.'

Tigran paused, smiling. 'I told him he was the chosen one and in his manic state he simply believed me.'

John groaned. Biro touched his arm. 'The chosen one!'

'Yes, that's right. I told him that I am John the Baptist and that he is the chosen son of God.'

'Jesus!'

'Exactly so.'

Biro could contain himself no longer. 'You're an evil fuck, Gevorkian!'

Tigran threw back his head and roared. It was hideous. Out of the corner of his eye John could see Biro tapping keys on his weblink.

'Don't waste your time, Biro. We have a shield up. You can't trace us.'

'But that's illegal!' John knew immediately it was an extremely stupid thing to say. He blushed. This was Tigran Gevorkian after all.

Biro shrugged and closed his link down.

'And you can call off your drones. They won't find us either.'

'Seems you know just what we're doing.'

'I do.'

John thought for a few seconds then decided to come right out with it. 'Why'd you want the algorithm?'

'Why not?'

'What can you do with it?'

'Nothing.'

'So why d'you want it?'

'Bargaining chip.'

'Bargaining for what?'

'Maybe money, John.' There was a pause. 'I'm going to leave you now. Talk to Susie. Tell her what the deal is.'

'I don't think…' He was gone. The screen was blank, black.

'Holy shit,' Biro exclaimed, banging his palm down on the desk.

John walked to the window and looked out across King's Parade. It was raining. 'What we gonna do, Biro?' He looked helpless. He felt helpless. 'Can't face telling Susie.'

'Well... I guess...'

'You guess, do you?' John was angry.

'Hey, John, don't take it out on me.'

John turned away from the window and looked at Biro. For all his hard exterior John could see he was hurt. 'I'm sorry, Biro. It's just that...'

'I know. I know, man.'

They stood looking at each other, trapped by their doubts and indecisions.

'What next, John?'

John's brain was racing, going through a host of possibilities. 'If we can't track him down we have to draw him out.'

'Maybe we can find him.'

'How?'

'You told me once that Felix had an electronic tag implanted so you could track him when he had a manic...'

'You're right, Biro. Brilliant. I dunno why that didn't occur to me.'

'Never mind that.'

'It was only a temporary thing. Might not function anymore.'

'It's worth a try even if Gevorkian has a shield up.'

'Of course.' John clicked a net connection. 'Mary, get me Dr Floyd, please.' John drummed his fingers on his desk, still feeling crushed and nervous. The screen lit up and Floyd appeared.

'Yes, John?'

'Can you try connecting to Felix's tag please?'

'I already have. No connection.'

'Thought that'd be the case, Doc, but thanks for trying.'

'I'm keeping the link open in case the situation changes.'

'Good.' John stood. 'I'm going to see the cops.'

'Is that wise?'

'It's a risk I'll have to take I guess. Might lead somewhere… probably not.'

Chapter Four
Cop Shop

There is no trap as deadly as the trap you set for yourself.
Raymond Chandler in *The Long Goodbye*

John and Biro walked over to the cop shop. They were standing in reception when John caught sight of Comb-over. He was taken aback and waved at him to catch his eye. Comb-over saw John and waved back, coming through to reception. They shook hands. He looked older and was completely bald. John last saw him when they left him naked on the moors with Tigran and his gang. They really had no choice. Comb-over had infiltrated the gang and had to play the part to the hilt.

'Bloody hell, Grimsthorne, I'd've thought you'd have retired by now!'

'I'm younger than I look, John.'

'Must be.'

He shook Biro's hand. 'Good to see you again, Biro. I'm told you're making successful films now.'

'S'right.'

'Come through to my office.' He led the way out of reception and into a spacious, well- furnished room.

Biro glanced around. 'Looks like you've come up in the

world.'

'Yes, well, I've had a few successes in the last 10 years, though I never did bust the Gevorkian mob.'

'Sorry I had to leave you like that.'

'Never mind, John. You did the right thing at the time.'

'Thanks.'

'So what brings you here?'

'Tigran Gevorkian.' He waited while Comb-over did a double-take.

'What!'

'Gevorkian.'

'You've seen him?'

'Only on a weblink. Not in person.'

'Where is he?'

'Wish we knew.'

'Why?'

'He's taken - kidnapped - our son Felix.'

Comb-over looked genuinely shocked. 'Why?'

'Wants his car back.'

'*What*! His car back! That's ridiculous.'

'Well, not just his car,

'What else?'

'An algorithm Susie's working on.'

'Which is?'

John looked away towards the window. 'I can't tell you.'

'Why not?'

'Because I don't really know.'

'Hasn't she told you?'

'No. It's, as they say, top secret.'

'Who's she working for?'

'Don't really know that either.'

'Any ideas?'

'The government maybe.'

'And…?'

'Something about the New World Order Movement.'

Comb-over was caught off guard. He stiffened noticeably. 'That's dangerous territory, John.'

'I know that, Grimsthorne.'

'Can I talk to her?'

Biro stepped in to fill the void. 'John hasn't told Susie yet that Tigran has Felix.'

'Why not?'

'We only found out this morning - just now.'

'So what you going to do, John?'

'Go home and tell her.'

Chapter Five
2030

In 2030 England had become more or less an island of the arts. There was virtually no manufacturing or industry. All that had, of course, moved to China and India. John and Susie had seen this coming. Powerful advances had been made in work with stem cells, cytokines and proteomics, knocking the wind out of the sales of Giant Pharma. Stem cell therapy had advanced in leaps and bounds. Text-messaging had gone out of fashion and people had started talking again. It was also possible to say hello to children in the street without being lynched!

Having said that, very little progress had been made in the understanding and treatment of mental illness. Consciousness itself remained as much a mystery to science as it did when Susie and John first met. Not so to the mystics. In 2011 there were 28 million Americans practising Hatha Yoga - by now the transcendent and enlightening powers of meditation had fully come into their own.

As Samuel Johnson once observed: "It was never supposed that cogitation is inherent in matter, or that every particle is a thinking being. Yet, if any part of matter be devoid of thought, what part can we suppose to think? Matter can differ from matter only in form, density, bulk, motion, and direction of motion: to which of these, however varied or combined, can consciousness be annexed? To be round or square, to be solid or fluid, to be great or little, to be moved slowly or swiftly one way or another, are modes of material existence, all equally alien from the nature of cogitation. If matter be once without thought, it can only be made to think by some new modification."

They had entered what Susie and John jokingly referred to as The Empire of the Saints. As Susie had predicted when they met, the smarter members of the science community had now accepted that blind chance was not the driving force behind the universe but rather that there was a design. It was understood that evolution was guided by what might be called a *blueprint*. Here we are, conscious beings, in a universe but we don't know how we got here, why we're here and what to do now we're here. It had always struck John that not only are we conscious like the animals, the insects and the fish but we are self-conscious - we are aware of our own existence. As Sir John Polkinghorne once observed, 'We know the stars but they know nothing'. You gotta wonder how consciousness rose up out of rock, mud and sunlight. And then self-consciousness - wow! You gotta wonder. What purpose does self-consciousness serve other than a knowing of the thing in itself by itself? And to what end? John wondered if it was like this so that we can know that we are God - that we are the infinite, eternal conscious Self - not the squirming little ego self but the big one. The Big Self that is everything and contains everything within itself.

By 2018 the wild mushroom Fly Agaric Amanita Muscaria, known as the Fly Agaric, had become more common and could be found in the autumn all over the British Isles. It is a basidiomycete fungus. In 2005 its use had become illegal. In 2020 this ruling had been reversed and it became permissible to trip on the mushroom. Apart from it being impossible to control the use of the mushroom due to its being readily available to one and all, it was also realised that unlike alcohol Fly Agaric did not lead to violent and anti-social behaviour but rather it increased empathy and had a calming and enlightening effect. It is also still used widely in the treatment of some mental illnesses.

With the advent of 3D printers people made a lot of what was required in their own homes. They were cheap as chips and the raw materials were made from plants, soil and rock. Using these printers desalination plants were constructed in vast numbers around the coastlines and then elegantly hidden underground. The collecting pipes were buried in the seabed and then fed to the plants. The pure water was then piped away underground to link up with local water supplies. The impending water wars had been prevented and no one in the world ever went without this essential again.

Following the introduction of many new sources of energy the demand for oil had dropped away so there was peace in the Middle East and America was no longer hell-bent on beating the living shit out of the territories she needed to control and exploit to satisfy her craving for the black goo.

Aside from nuclear fusion by far the most significant development were the quantum vacuum zero-point energy machines, based on electromagnetic waves which exist only in the vacuum of empty space. These waves constitute an ocean of infinite energy, which can be coaxed to pour into our 3-dimensional world from their 4-dimensional realm, providing electricity to power all transport, to heal the body of almost all disease and to create weapons of enormous and unimaginable power. The discovery of Scalar Electromagnetics - the zero point energy, the energy of the absolute nothingness which existed before the universe came into being - was made by a Serb called Nikola Tesla in the late 19th and early 20th century. He was an essential driving force in the birth of commercial electricity. Tesla was 86 when he died - completely forgotten and with no money - in a hotel in New York City.

A heavy chest containing a 47 gram metal alloy idol was given to CIA officials for safekeeping at Lo Monthang (called *Mustang* in CIA files) by a Tibetan monk accompanied by Khampa bodyguards in 1959. The chest was kept in a CIA store-room in Washington DC labelled *St Circus Mustang-0183* in the army base of Camp Hale near Vail, Colorado. When they opened the chest an ancient manuscript was found with an idol inside.

The chest was magnificent. The heavy metal-lined wooden chest had a socket-and-pivot hinged lid and an ancient loop-and-rod lock assembly. It was a cubical box eight inches square of teak and was six inches thick and lined with a one inch bronze-like alloy plate. It was a work of great expertise and its condition indicated that it had lain buried for a considerable period of time.

The manuscript was in pre-Rigvedic Sanskrit. The manuscript told the name of the idol, Kalpa Maha-Ayusham Rasayana Vigraha.

The section of most interest to the CIA was the Sudarshana Chakra, which was created by the combined energy of Brahma, Vishnu and Mahesh. This chakra is a spinning disc with 108 serrations. It is a weapon that is controlled by the mind and the weapon can only be activated by the mantra only known to the owner. Chakra Scalar Electromagnetic Interferometry works through the mind and can produce a scalar electromagnetic wave, which can lock onto any other scalar phenomena and influence it. The scalar component of the electromagnetic wave are activated by opposing electromagnetic waves - a wave and its anti-wave. The waves cancel each other's electrical and magnetic fields and the result is an electromagnetic scalar wave, the Sudarshan Chakra, will follow the mind commands of the owner. In the scalar interferometry mode it becomes a terribly destructive weapon its waves travelling faster than light.

Nikola Tesla was introduced to this weapon by Swami Vivekananda. As a spinning howitzer it operates in the exothermic and endothermic mode. In endothermic mode the howitzer sucks energy out of the target area, creating a blast of deep cold at the distant target, which could freeze an ocean.

Using the exothermic and cold endothermic modes together weather can be altered anywhere. Warm the air over here, cool it down over there, put a curl in the jet stream, dissipate and create clouds and tornados. In this mode it could fry anything selectively. In the frightening Psychotronic mode it affects the electromagnetic mind-body connection causing loss of consciousness, leaving the mind highly susceptible to suggestions. To his credit Vishnu never used the Sudarshan Chakra weapon to its full potential, even when provoked.

Of course there had been enormous resistance to new energy sources from the Petrodollar countries particularly the USA and Saudi Arabia. There had been threats, but public pressure and the demand for energy had prevented serious conflict. As a consequence the USA was reverting fast to its agricultural roots. More and more people had turned to vegetarianism as the world population had exploded and pressure on the land had increased beyond the most pessimistic predictions. It was a practical necessity and was not sparked so much by sensitivity to animal welfare and suffering but by hunger. And this was working on the local level and organically, cutting down on wastage and transportation costs. A method had been developed to process human waste for fertiliser, cleaning and purifying it to rid the waste matter of harmful drug residues.

Intelligent, caring people had woken up to the glaringly obvious fact that all animal agriculture involved violence, suffering and death, including even the most humanely produced milk, cheese and eggs. Male chicks had been ground up alive or pounded or gassed to death. They were of no use to the farmers and had to die as soon as they were born. Yikes! One of the worst things in the world is the sound of cows when their babies are taken from them. In a conventional dairy the calves were taken away the same day or the next day. In an organic dairy, which is a supposedly higher-level animal welfare 'happy place', they were taken away two or three days later. The mothers cried for days. The fact that we would take a cow with a natural life span of 30 years, impregnate her six times and take away her babies six times and kill her after she has had mastitis for five years was dreadful. This was the mechanisation of the reproductive processes of a female cow, the commodification of a mother and her baby. The reproductive process and the relationship of a mother and her child became a product.

Gone were the fat-cat corporate conglomerate food producers. In 2011 when John and Susie married 150 million people went to bed hungry – that's one in eight members of the human race. That had to change. And it did. The idea of the goal of endless economic and industrial growth had finally gone out of fashion as it dawned on the human race that we live on a finite planet with decidedly finite resources. We had finally woken up. In the UK Christianity was more or less off the radar just as the idea that Jesus Christ was the only son of God had found its true perspective.

Much power had been leeched away from the banks and the international corporations as their corruption and scandalous exploitation had been slowly but surely exposed. Fat-cat bonuses paid to CEOs and senior managers for doing next to nothing were a thing of the past. Wealth was now more equally distributed though there remained considerable imbalance. Human greed still played its part of course but most excesses had been controlled and held in check by the sheer weight of public outrage and pressure. Having said that, the Federal Reserve under the thumb of the Illuminati still wielded considerable power over the flow and control of so-called 'money'. The New World Order Movement had gathered huge numbers of followers and had gone from strength to strength. Many people were waiting for them to show their hand. Especially Susie. It was of more concern to her than it was to John, caught up in his infatuation with art and film.

The radical Islamic movement ISIS had pushed the boat out too far and burnt itself out by 2020 - with the help of NATO air power of course. The blood-curdling beheadings of their enemies eventually turned world public opinion against them. It was hard on peaceful Muslims but they hung in and were eventually completely integrated and accepted into 'Western' society.

Russia was assimilated into European Union in 2025. So there were no longer any tensions or power games on that front. Well, not much anyway. The world had woken up. Global warming had ceased and as under control at the time of writing.

Growth. Back in 2011 John, Susie and Biro were on a boat heading back to shore having dumped John's desktop and the two guns in the ocean. John had written about this adventure in his book *Nothing and Everywhere*. Susie and John were on the bridge with the captain. Radio 4 was on air and a correspondent was discussing growth and the importance of the UK growing the economy. Susie threw a V-sign at the radio. She looked upset and John asked her what was bothering her. Their conversation went something like this:

"The ludicrous and dangerous stupidity of capitalism," Susie expounded, "is that it leads to the idea that economies and industries can grow and grow and grow. This is nonsense to anyone with half a brain. Growth can't just go on and on and on. If it did we would just grow ourselves right off the planet. On top of that resources are obviously finite. There's only so much we can take before the whole thing runs dry and we plough right into the ground. Whifflediff! End of story. Get it?"

"Yeah, I get it," John replied and added, "and my guess is that this has something to do with mathematics. Am I right?"

"You are and it does, John."

"Go on then. I know you're dying to tell me."

"There's a book," she told John, "called *Limits to Growth*, which examined the past thirty years of reality with the predictions made in 1972 and which found that changes in industrial and food production, and pollution are all in line with the book's position. These predictions were based on math principles and formulae. The scary thing is that the book predicted economic and societal collapse in the twenty first century - where we are right now."

She turned to the captain. "Have you got a sheet of paper and a pencil I could use, please?"

"Sure." He opened a draw beside him and pulled out a

notebook and a felt tip pen. "Here."

"Thanks." She leaned forward over a small worktop and started to write. John watched in a kind of enchanted way. She turned and handed the notebook to John. He looked at it intently and this is what he read:

$$y = \frac{\log(1- (1 - g)\, x_c) - 1}{\log(g)}$$

Susie watched over John's shoulder. "This is the formula for calculating the amount of time left for a resource straining under the lash of constant growth."

"Doesn't mean diddlysquat to me."

"Didn't think it would, John. I just wanted you to see what just a few little symbols can do to explain big and very complicated things."

Artificial Intelligence. The quest for full AI that would work just like the human brain/mind had come to nothing and development ceased in 2020. It turned out be unattainable. There had always been a fear that robots would come to rival human beings and this had dampened enthusiasm for the project. However they made full use of household and manufacturing robots. It took away so much of the drudgery of cleaning and boring, repetitive tasks, which was to the good. The search for full AI was outlawed worldwide and all research was terminated or limited to only the manufacturing of programmable utility machines. By 2020 driverless cars, aircraft, ships, trains and 'copters were well established and did the work. Lithium-ion rechargeable batteries, which stored solar energy, were commonplace and not just during power outages.

Antibiotics. Overuse had led to a weakening of the effectiveness of these drugs and it came to be fully appreciated that all drugs and medications were derived from nature. Huge amounts of labour, resources and money had been poured into R&D and at the time of writing they had powerful treatments and cures for even the most intractable diseases and other ailments. Indian, Tibetan and Chinese natural cures had played a big part in the advances. These natural medicines worked without the terrible side effects of man-made concoctions, which more often than not had made things worse for sufferers and led to greater and greater dependency.

Nanotechnology. Scientists working in the field of nanotechnology looked to nature to provide ideas for smart ways to solve complex problems. They studied spider silk and lotus leaves to replicate their special properties like their tensile strength or ability to repel water in engineered materials. Nanotechnology works because electrons do not exist in a single fixed state but can simultaneously exist in many states at once.

Quantum computing came next. The difference between old fashioned computing and quantum computing is the qubit. A qubit or quantum bit is a unit of quantum information - the quantum analogue of the classical bit. A qubit is a two-state quantum-mechanical system. In the classical system a bit would have to be in one state or the other. Quantum mechanics however allows the qubit to be in a superposition of both states at the same time. This is the very essence of quantum computing. Scientists came up with a whole new toolkit with the potential to change almost everything from unimaginably small computer chips to tiny machines that could find and fix damaged arteries and could even repair damaged DNA. Indeed, DNA computers were developed. Nanotechnology made clean energy cleaner too.

You may wonder, dear reader, how I know so much about the future and you will find out how later on in this book. I have opted to tell this story in the third person, which you may find strange but isn't life itself strange and deeply mysterious? Anyway I believe that writing it in the third person makes it more accessible. I may be wrong of course but

I leave that to you to judge.

Chapter Six

Jesus Saves

God is a mathematician.
Gottfried Wilhelm von Leibniz

'When can I go out into the world to spread my message?'

'Not yet, my Lord. The time is not right.'

Tigran and Felix were standing in a large, almost bare, windowless room. There were two chairs. The walls and ceiling were clad in salt and three inch deep crystals covered the floor. Air infused with fine particles of salt chugged into the room. They were wearing white robes. Tigran looked surprisingly like a Jewish mystic.

'When will the time be right?'

'I am waiting for a sign.'

'But I am ready and I am the Lord.'

'And *I* baptized you, my Lord. *I* came before you.' There was a knock on the door.

'Enter.' A burly Russian looking man stood in the doorway.

'Word, boss?'

'Go ahead, Seaweed.'

'In… private.'

Tigran followed Seaweed out of the room. Felix sat down

and stared at the wall. White on white.

Seaweed led Tigran into a comfortable sitting room with deep, brown leather chairs and enormous glass tanks populated by brightly coloured fish. It was tranquil and very quiet.

'There's some activity on the surface, boss.'

'What's happening?'

'Patrols are more frequent and they're hangin' about?'

Tigran walked to a control console and flicked a switch. Several monitors lit up, showing fields and a small wood. Men and women in blue uniforms appeared to be scouring through the undergrowth.

'What do *you* make of it, boss?'

'I'd say without a doubt they're looking for the boy downstairs and just happen to be poking around here. It's a coincidence. That's all.'

'When you gonna trade him?'

'Not yet. Let 'em sweat it.'

'The longer we keep him the more likely they are to find us. Aren't you taking a bigger risk?'

'All life is a risk, Seaweed.'

He thought about this. 'Well, sure. But tell me what it is exactly that you want from 'em?'

'I've told you, my car.'

'Can't believe it's just that, boss. Too much risk... for that.'

'OK. It's not just that now.'

'What's happened?'

'The boy told me his mother's working on an algorithm that'll be used to penetrate the New World Order Movement firewalls and go right to its heart.

'Sorry.'

'What?'

'Algorithm?'

'Ah. You could say it's a formula for solving a problem.'

'Who's she working for?'

'Not sure.'

'Could be she won't want to let you have the...'

'Algorithm.'

'Yeah, algorithm.'

'You're right. She probably won't.'

'And maybe she won't be free to let you have it even if she wanted.'

'That's also a reasonable assessment of the situation.'

'She'll certainly be between a rock and a hard place.

'We need the money. We gotta push it.'

'There must be other ways.'

'What are you driving at, Seaweed?'

'Driving at the hard place.'

'Hard place!'

'Where we're going...'

'You getting' soft on me?'

'No, but...'

'But, but. but! Go away. Find something useful to do and leave me to think.'

Seaweed looked crushed, humiliated. He left the room, shrunken. Gevorkian went back to studying the monitors. The area above him looked clear. It seemed the search was over. He was pleased with himself. He sat down and closed his eyes.

In the salt room Felix was pacing to and fro. He was agitated. He paused, staring down at his feet. He pushed his toes through the salt forming a small hill, which he endeavored to shape into a pyramid and with some success then sat down in the salt and said to himself, 'Solving the quantum measurement problem requires a revolutionary change in how we understand the relationship between our mental and physical states. The physical world has none of the familiar physical properties that we take it to have. The world that we observe is created by our mental state, which relates directly to our physical state. Simple!'

He lay down on the salt. He had calmed and he said, 'I am what I am and I am He. I am the Creator, the preserver and the destroyer of worlds. All is within me and everything is me. I am this. I am that - all and everything in all times and in all places. I see the world in a grain of salt. I see worlds within worlds whirling into and out of themselves - without beginning, without end. Come unto me and I will reveal your Self to yourself. I am you.'

Susie was sitting in the garden dozing when John reached home. Biro had gone back to their office, angry and helpless. John pulled a deckchair across the grass to sit next to her under the shade of an apple tree. He kissed her and took her hand.

'We know where he is.'

Susie sat bolt upright, giving John her full attention. She looked tired and drained.

'Prepare yourself.'

She pressed her hands together almost in prayer.

'Felix has been kidnapped.'

'What! Why?'

'You're going to find this difficult to believe.'

'Try me.'

'He's been taken by Tigran Gevorkian.'

Susie was struck dumb. John waited for her to recover. 'He's OK. We've spoken to Gevorkian on Starscan.'

'How d'you know he's OK?'

'Because Gevorkian is using him as a bargaining chip.'

Bargaining chip! What's he bargaining for?'

'His car.'

'That can't be all.'

'It isn't.'

'So what else?'

'Your algorithm.'

'What algorithm?'

'The one you're working on for the Consortium.'

'But it's not mine, John.'

'You created it.'

'Yes, I did. But it's not mine to bargain with. And anyway it's too important, too powerful…'

Their Starscan link sounded. They both jumped to their feet, ran into the house and through to the sitting-room. They stopped dead in their tracks when they saw Felix looking out at them from the big screen.

Susie lunged forwards. 'Felix!'

'Hello.'

'Where are you?

'I don't know.'

'But you're a prisoner.'

'Am I?'

'Yes, you are.'

'I don't feel imprisoned.'

John walked to Susie's side. 'But this room you're in… it's all white. What is it?'

'Just a room. A salt room.'

'What d'you mean, a salt room?'

'Floor's salt, wall's salt, ceiling's salt.'

'And you're wearing white.'

'Correct.'

They were both lost for words.

Felix broke the silence, 'I and my Father are one. I am the way, the truth, and the life: no man cometh unto the Father but by me.'

'Jesus!'

'Yes, you're close.' He paused. 'I am the one.'

John was starting to heat up. 'The one *what*?'

'The chosen son of God, come into the world again to save mankind from descent into the abyss.'

'What are you talking about, Felix?'

Susie took up the challenge. 'I gave birth to you Felix. *I* know who you are.'

'Do you?'

'Yes, I do. You are our son, Felix.'

'I am not.'

'Who are you then?'

'I am what I am.'

'Which is?'

'The son of God.'

'We're all children of God,' John interjected.

'Not in the way I am.'

'Don't be silly. You're muddled. You're not well.'

'I am not muddled and I am well.'

John shrugged. He was giving up.

But not Susie. 'Why are you wearing that robe, Felix?'

'He gave it to me.'

'Who is he?'

'John.'

'John?'

'Not you. John the Baptist.'

'I can't take anymore.' John turned his back on the screen and walked away.

'Don't go. We have to stay with this.'

'I can't stay with it.'

Gevorkian stepped into the picture also wearing a white robe. 'I will contact you again in ten minutes.' The screen went black and Susie immediately picked up a web-phone. 'I must call the Consortium.'

'No, Susie, don't do that. Not yet. Let's wait to hear what he has to say.'

'OK. OK, You're right. We'll do that.' Susie paced the room. John slumped in a chair. It started to rain heavily. Water streamed down the picture window and drummed on the roof. It felt appropriate. Every minute or so Susie glanced at her watch. 'The Consortium would never agree to me sharing even a small part of the algorithm with anyone, especially with a crook like Gevorkian.'

'So what do we do if that's what he's demanding?'

'We string him along. Keep the door open. Negotiate. And, anyway, the algorithm isn't completed yet.'

'I didn't appreciate that.'

'It was neither here nor there.'

'So just what do we say when he reconnects?'

'We tell him that I will speak to the Consortium.'

'He won't like that. He wants to keep it between the two of

you. He knows you have access to the thing and that you could give it to him.'

'That's true, John.'

'So you must come up with a reason why you cannot let him have it.'

'I can't think of one.'

'Encryption? Cipher-text?'

'Same thing, John.'

The screen lit up again. Tigran appeared alone.

'What have you decided?'

John stood. 'We haven't.'

Susie stood. 'As things stand I'm not in a position to let you have it, Gevorkian.'

'Why not?'

'Because it's on the Consortium's mainframe and I don't have access to that.'

'But it's *your* work.'

'True. But it belongs to them.'

'And what is this… Consortium?'

'It's an independent group committed to work against the New World Order Movement.'

'And who's their leader?'

'There is no leader. We're equals.'

'I don't believe you?'

'Don't believe what?'

'That you don't have access to your work. You must have a copy.'

'No, I don't.'

'I don't buy that.'

'Well, that's your tough shit, Gevorkian. You can believe what you want. Facts are facts.'

'You will *have* to get it.'

'Or what?'

'I will let Felix loose on the world.'

'If you do that we'll find him.'

'Maybe not.'

'How come?'

'Wait and see… or get me the algorithm. It's up to you, Susie Bellavista.'

'I haven't completed it yet!'

The screen went blank. He was gone. Susie and John looked at each other, lost for words. John broke the silence. 'I presume you do have a copy of the algorithm as far as it goes.'

'Of course.'

'Thought so. You were very convincing.'

'Had to be.'

They lapsed into silence again then Susie stood. 'I'm going to the lab. Maybe we can find a way to penetrate Gevorkian's shield.'

'D'you think there might be?'

'It's more than possible that we'll find something in the archives. Data like that is mostly stored. Anyway I live in hope.' She walked to the door. 'See you later.'

Chapter Seven
Where Are Your Memories When You're Not Remembering Them?

We humans and all the matter of the universe are connected to the furthest reaches of the cosmos through Zero Point Field Waves.

Hal Puthoff

Susie was sitting at a bench surrounded by monitors, touch screens and paperwork. She was writing in a note-book with a pencil.

'Andy, can you pull the file for April 2003, please?'

Dr Andy Macadam, a young man with red hair wearing a white overall, pushed his trolley down an aisle and stopped by a filing shelf. He was a first class mathematician, who was always seeking to work with Susie. He relished being in her company. She enthralled and inspired him.

He studied the folders on display then pulled one out and laid it on his trolley, which he pushed up to Susie's bench. He handed the folder to her. She took it, opened it up and started going through the contents. Andy waited for further instructions. Susie looked up at him and smiled. Andy blushed, touching Susie's heart.

'Take a break, Andy. I'll give you a call when I need you again.'

'Thanks, Professor. I'll be in the canteen.'

Susie watched him leave absent-mindedly. She was deep in thought. Her weblink buzzed. She took the call.

'Hi, John…No, I haven't found anything yet but I live in hope…It's all paperwork. Nothing on the system, which is strange. Are you at work? … OK.' Susie went back to the file, slowly going through it.

John arrived at the King's Parade office and joined Biro in the production suite where he was running a meeting with the prep crew. There was a big still photograph projected on the wall. Biro was pointing out features. John didn't interrupt the briefing.

'We'll set up the production compound on this flat river bed. It's ideal and has good access along this road here.' Biro swept his hand over the picture. 'It's rough but it'll be OK to get the initial team in, then we can improve the surface back to what serves as a main road. It's tarmacked up to a point. There're some deep gashes that we'll need to fill.' Biro glanced at John, who nodded and smiled weakly. Biro seemed satisfied and continued.

John went through to his office and over to the bookcase. He still preferred reading printed books as opposed to electronic versions. He pulled out a book about the life of

Mahatma Gandhi and opened it at random. He read: *"As human beings, our greatness lies not so much in being able to remake the world – that is the myth of the atomic age – as in being able to remake ourselves. If you change yourself you will change your world. If you change how you think then you will change how you feel and what actions you take. And so the world around you will change. Not only because you are now viewing your environment through new lenses of thoughts and emotions but also because the change within can allow you to take action in ways you wouldn't have – or maybe even have thought about – while stuck in your old thought patterns."*

Gandhi never failed to hit the spot. His non-violent revolution helped to kick out the Brits and liberate his country from imperial bondage and exploitation. Quite a man!

John stood watching the stream of students, shoppers and merchants passing under his window. He had been in some very tight spots before but this one took the biscuit. He waited for a flash of insight or a glimmer of hope but neither came. There was a warning knock on his door and Biro came in.

'John, we've got a problem in Afghan.' He paused.

'Yes?'

'The stills cameraman I left out there - Patrice. D'you remember him?'

'Of course.'

Biro came to stand beside John at the window. 'He's dead.'

'What!'

'Dead.'

'How?'

'Looks like he was murdered.'

'Holy shit!'

'My sentiments exactly, John.'

'So… what's happening?'

'The tribal elders are onto it and there are some cops coming out from Kabul.'

'Waste of time.'

'The cops?'

'Yes.'

'The elders will get to the bottom of it and sort it out.'

'OK, Biro but one of us should get out there to represent the company and sort out the return of his body to France.'

'Agreed, but under the circumstances that can't be you.'

'It's gonna be you then.'

'S'right. I'll be a quick as I can. You need me here.'

John nodded his agreement. 'Susie's in the uni tech archives to see if she can find a way to bust the shield.'

'Illegal, John.'

John shrugged. 'Got to meet the evil with the devil in this case, Biro, old buddy.'

'I guess.' Biro punched a code into his comslink. 'Book me on the next flight out of Heathrow to Afghanistan, please. And send a 'copter over when I need to leave. Let me know... thanks.' Biro turned back to the window. 'This view never fails to impress me and lift me up.' He was looking across at King's College chapel, beautiful in the setting afternoon sun.

As John turned back into the room Susie appeared on the wall-screen. 'It looks like we've got something here, boys.' She held up shiny plastic disc. 'Right now we're looking for a machine to play this on. They heard a voice off, 'I think I've tracked one down in London at the Science Museum.'

Susie walked out of shot. Biro gave John a thumbs-up. 'Gonna pack a bag. See ya in a coupla days.'

'Good luck, man.'

'Likewise.' Biro smiled and left the office. John nodded to the comslink. 'Get me the Foreign Office, please, Mary. Jock Anderson.' John waited. Jock appeared on the wall-screen. 'How're things, John?'

'Not too good. How 'bout you.'

'OK, thanks. So what's up?'

'Got a problem out in Afghan. One of our camera team is dead. It looks like he was murdered.'

'Is he one of ours?'

'D'you mean is he *British*?

'Yup.'

'No he's not. He's French.'

'Well…'

'Come on, Jock. He was on our team just like you.'

'OK, OK, John. What's his name?

'Patrice Roubinet.'

'Where's he live?'

'Apartment in Paris but he's hardly ever there.'

'Why's that?'

'Obvious isn't it?'

'No.'

John sighed. 'He works for us, Jock.'

'Ah, yes. Got you.'

'OK. Biro's flying out today but please go right ahead and find out whatever you can.'

'I'll get the team onto it.'

'Thanks…there's one more thing…'

'Yes?'

'Can you check with Afghan immigration to see if any Armenians or Russians have come into the country or left it in the last day?'

'Sure. But why?'

'It's a long story and I don't want to tell it now.'

'Fair enough but the Afghans are notoriously inept at keeping or locating records.'

'I know that, Jock, I've been there a few times. Just give it a go, please.'

'Will do, John. 'Bye now.'

'Bye, Jock.'

John punched a key and Susie came up on his wall-screen.

'Hi, John. No good news I guess.'

'You're right 'bout that... but some bad news.'

'Oh no.'

'Not about Felix. Well apparently not... maybe...'

'What're you driving at, John?'

He couldn't decide how to approach the issue in the best way so he just came straight to the point. 'Patrice is dead.'

'Patrice Roubinet?'

'Yes. He died in Afghan and it seems like he might have been murdered. Facts are hard to come by.'

'So what're you doing?'

'Biro's flying out today…'

'And?'

'I called Jock Anderson at the Foreign Office and asked him to find out what the fuck was going on.'

'Will he?'

'Sure, Susie, he owes us plenty for all those fat consultancy fees.'

'That machine we tracked down at the Science Museum has been disabled. It's only for show. We're gonna have to rebuild it.'

'How long?'

'There's the rub. A coupla days minimum with even the very best 3D printer nerds on the case. Some parts have to be created and printed from scratch using the drawings.'

'This is getting... another two days!'

'Hope and pray.'

Chapter Eight
The Empire of the Saints

A lot of power comes with being a mystic.
They can be corrupted by money and sex.

Andrew Rawlinson

Word had reached John that his Guru, Swami Sat Chit Ananda, was in town. He was ninety two years old and still going *strong*. John had called his hotel in London to set up an appointment. He wanted to get Swami Ji's take on the situation with Gevorkian and the algorithm. John travelled to the city in an unmanned 'copter and was let down into the park near where Swami Ji was staying.

As John flew he recalled Eknath Easwaran saying to him once in LA that only a few centuries ago bright people all over Europe believed that the sun, stars and planets orbited around the earth. Some of the greatest geniuses in the West - Archimedes, Plato, Aristotle and Dante - were absolutely certain that the earth was the centre of the universe. It took one man, Copernicus, to knock the bottom out of this theory. As he wrote, *today we know that the sun not the earth is the centre of the solar system and that even the sun is but one of billions in a galaxy that is among billions of galaxies. But if we look inside ourselves we find to our consternation that each of us believes that we are at the centre of the world. In fact of course it is God who is at the centre and this centre is in the very depths of our own consciousness.*

John met Swami Ji in the hotel lounge, which was empty apart from the two of them. He was waiting for John. He was dressed all in white, looking as noble and beautiful as ever. He always inspired and brought out the love in John's heart. John bowed and, with a benign smile, Swami Ji gestured for him to sit down.

'Thank you so much for agreeing to speak to me, Swami Ji.'

'There is no need to thank me, John. I am always at your service.'

'You are too kind, Sir.' John bowed again. 'Are you well?' The sage looked well but he had to ask. Politeness.

He smiled again as John sat.

'I am well but you are looking worried. So, John, what's on your mind?'

'I'm in turmoil. Susie and I are in a very painful and difficult position and we don't know what to do to resolve the problem.'

'And what is the problem?'

'It's this: our son Felix has been kidnapped and the criminal who took him is demanding a ransom that we cannot pay. His name is Tigran Gevorkian.'

'I understood that you are now a wealthy man.'

'The kidnapper does not want money, Swami Ji, He wants something that we cannot give him.'

'And that is?'

'A mathematical formula - an algorithm.'

'Why does he want this algorithm?'

'He wants to sell it to some...organisation.'

'Which is?'

'The New World Order Movement.'

'Ah. I begin to understand your problem'.

'Good.'

'Remember though, John, that I am your spiritual guide and that I cannot sort out issues of a personal nature.'

'I am aware of that, Swami Ji. But I would appreciate your guidance on how we should proceed.'

'All right, John. Why can't you give this man the algorithm?'

'Because it's not ours to give. It belongs to the Consortium which hired Susie to produce it. However, although her work isn't finished, she *could* give it to them when it is complete.'

'Clearly you cannot give away something that is not yours to give but it is nonetheless of great importance to free your son.'

'It certainly is. Especially so because Felix is in the midst of a manic episode and the kidnappers have managed to convince him that he is Jesus Christ and that he - the kidnapper - is John the Baptist.'

Swami Ji appeared a little taken aback as he sought to grasp the full meaning of what John was telling him. They sat in silence for a few minutes. John was happy just to look at him. Eventually he looked John in the eye and asked, 'Is it not possible for the police to help you?'

'No, they can't help, Swami Ji.'

'Why not?'

'Because Gevorkian is hiding behind a shield.'

'But they're illegal, John.'

'True. But then so is kidnapping and extortion.'

'What it boils down to is that we cannot find him or our son but Susie is searching through the university archives for a way to locate the shield and penetrate it.'

'That sounds... promising.'

'Yes, it is, Swami Ji. But getting inside the shield is only half the battle.'

'And the other half is?'

'Bargaining for Felix's freedom without supplying the

algorithm.'

'That is, as they say, a tall order, John.'

'Indeed it is, Swami Ji.'

He was silent again for a minute or so and then he said, 'Before you meditate ask the Lord for a solution.'

'Is it that simple?'

'Yes, John. That's it. The Lord will provide.'

John wasn't too sure about this but he said he would certainly give it a try. As he left the hotel he pondered on Swami Ji's words and concluded that nature, God, call it what you will, does most things without him doing anything. His digestive system, for instance. His respiratory system. His nervous system. His brain itself. They do their own thing regardless of him. He doesn't do them. He didn't make himself. He was made. There it is.

John walked on. He could see the 'copter approaching silently. Then it hit him. Simple. Gevorkian suddenly didn't seem so bright. It had just not occurred to him that once Susie had completed the algorithm she could use it before handing it over to him. Of course he had to admit that it hadn't occurred to them either. He guessed that they were just too spaced out and frightened to think the thing through. He climbed aboard the 'copter and headed back to Cambridge.

John attempted to connect with Susie as they sped along but didn't reach her immediately, which was irritating.

As the spires of Cambridge swam into view the comslink finally came alive and Susie appeared on the 'copter's screen. 'Hi.'

'Hello, Susie. What's happening?'

'Not a lot, John. How'd it go with Swami Ji?'

'It was great to see him, of course. He looked older, but well and was his usual inspiring self.'

'Did he suggest anything?'

'Not exactly, but he was encouraging.'

Susie didn't respond, so John took the bull by the horns. 'There's another thing…'

'Yes?'

'Uhm…'

'Yes?'

'Well, the penny's dropped.'

'What penny, John?'

'I can't believe that this didn't occur to us…or to Gevorkian come to that.'

'What, John?'

'That you could use the algorithm before we hand it over to him.'

'No. Can't be done. Not that simple.'

'Why?'

'Because the algorithm will show, shall we say, usage. It'll get embedded in the program itself. Take a million years to get it out. We'd need to work with it for too long to get right inside their world and find out everything they're up to, what their intentions are...'

'OK. So what's our next move?'

'Stall him with promises of a delivery while we work on locating and penetrating the shield.'

'When'll you be ready to have a go?'

'Tomorrow.'

'That's good. Just can't handle thinking about Felix in his state and being in that shit's hands.'

'At least he's under lock and key and can't do anything that'll get him into trouble.'

'Not so sure about that. He could become... difficult for Gevorkian to handle. And...'

'What, John?'

'I wonder if there's any connection between Patrice's death - murder - and Gevorkian.'

'I guess there could be. Does Gevorkian have connections in Afghan?'

'He'd have connections everywhere in that underworld I should think, Susie.'

"You're probably right. That connection's a real possibility. When d'you expect to hear from Biro?'

'Any time now.' The 'copter was set down on their King's Parade office rooftop. 'I'm at the office so I'll try him now.'

'OK. I'll get back to work. The sooner we can break into the shield the better for all of us.'

'All right, Susie. I'll leave you to it. I'll call you if I get through to Biro.'

John climbed out of the 'copter and walked down to his office. He went into reception. 'Any news?'

'We got a message to say he'll come on stream at five.'

John glanced at his watch. Two minutes to five. 'I'll be in my office.' As soon as he sat down at his desk the big wall-screen lit up and there was Biro looking hot and dusty.

'What news?'

'He was murdered.'

'How can you be sure?'

'Shot in the back of the head, John.'

John's com-link buzzed. 'Hang on, Biro.'

'Hello.'

'Jock here.'

'And?'

'Two Eastern European men entered Afghanistan four days ago. The Afghan immigration department have been very helpful. They sent us the passport details and they were forged. Seems like you might be onto something, John.'

'Can you have them held in Afghan?'

'I certainly can if they haven't already got out of the country.'

'Thanks, Jock. 'Bye. D'you hear that, Biro?'

'Sure did'.

'So it seems that Gevorkian is likely behind the murder'.

'Looks like it, John'.

'Throws a different light on the kidnap, doesn't it?

'Yes, of course but what does it mean?'

'Means he's putting the squeeze on us - making us feel the pressure'.

'It fuckin' sucks that Patrice had to die for *this*'.

'It does, Biro'.

'I'm gonna get Gevorkian and teach that fuck a lesson'.

'Revenge is futile, my friend'.

'Futile, yes, but satisfying, John. As we used to say in the army, payback is a mother-fucker'.

'So who's the one who's fucked?'

'Both parties. The done to *and* the done by. Both'.

'Sounds 'bout right, Biro.' There was a pause in the conversation while they let this news settle. 'Susie says she should have things set up to have an attempt to crack the shield tomorrow'.

'Will it work?'

'No telling but you know Susie. She's usually right about things'. John managed a croaky laugh.

'True, John. She sure knows her stuff.'

'One of the reasons I love her'.

'I'd best get back there, John, before Susie presses the button. I'll get a team together if we're going to assault his lair. I can see there's a Lightcruiser flight right through to Heathrow in two hours. I can make that if I use the stand-by 'copter. If all goes according to plan I can be back in Cambridge in seven hours. I'll gather some good people together during the ride to the airport. Better get going.'

'No guns, Biro.'

'Got that, boss.'

'OK. See you soon'.

'Not if I see you first.'

'Gallipoli - the film?'

'Right.'

John connected with Susie and told her what Jock had said and that Biro was heading home for the showdown.

'I told him no guns.'

'So what will they use, John?'

'Sticks and stones I guess.'

'And?'

'And what?'

'And what else?'

'Fists and knees.'

'Right, John.'

Susie was silent for a few seconds then asked, 'Should we tell Comb-over what we're planning?'

John took his time to answer. 'I think not.'

'But if we don't and we're exposed we could be in a shit-load of trouble.'

'I shouldn't worry 'bout that. Biro's an old hand at covering tracks and creating diversions. But I'll think about what you asked. Promise.'

'Empire of the saints, John, my love.'

Susie signed off and John sat at his desk twiddling his thumbs while he thought things through. They had no idea what Gevorkian would do when his shield was penetrated - if it ever was. Would he be caught off guard? Would he stand

and fight or make a run for it? And what about Felix? Could they ensure his safety if there was a fight with sticks and stones?

Chapter Nine
Screw You and the Horse You Came In On

If a tree falls in the forest and there are no living creatures there to hear it does it make a sound?

A few years earlier John was having lunch in Cambridge with David Dudley, Professor of Cognitive Science and Computer Science at the University of California. They ordered coffee and Donald looked hard at John.

'The weirdest thing about quantum mechanics, John, is the measurement problem. This is because the act of measurement involves our minds and those minds play an active role, affecting the measurement itself. The central feature of quantum theory that's puzzled theorists for decades is the critical role of observation. You see, when an atom or electron isn't observed it has no definite position or momentum. Instead it's in a superposition of countless possible positions or momenta. Only when the atom or electron is observed does it have a measured position or momentum. For many of us theorists the puzzle is that this behaviour of quantum objects seems so different to the behaviour of everyday objects like footballs. After all, they point out, a football, unlike an electron, does have a position, a momentum, a 3D shape, a colour, and other such properties, whether or not the football is observed. Why should observation be critical to electrons but not footballs?'

'Dunno, Dave. Tell me. I'm sure you want to.'

'I do and I will.' He laughed. 'The puzzle isn't the strangeness of electrons but a misconception about footballs. A football no more has a position or momentum when it's not observed than does an electron. Only in the act of observation do we construct a phenomenal football with a position, motion, colour, and shape. Only in the act of measurement by observation is an electron constructed with a position, or momentum. All phenomena are constructed by observation, whether quantum phenomena or football phenomena. Are you with me, John?'

'I'm OK. Just about keeping up with you.'

'Right. So every phenomenon we observe in nature is nothing but the creation of our minds, the invention of our consciousness. If we see it, we construct it. Got it?'

'Yup. Got it.' John thought about this for a minute or so. 'Sounds to me, Dave, like what the mystics teach - that the physical, observable universe is an illusion.'

'It is indeed, John. Solving the quantum measurement problem requires us to say how and why observers become involved in the construction of the determinate world in which we find ourselves. Physicists find themselves forced to talk about the relationship between mental and physical states in order to make quantum mechanics clear.'

'And so we must be co-creating our reality with everyone else. Yes?'

'Just so, John. You see the equilibrium at the central vector is growing, John, in perfect fractal octaves from the infinitely big to the infinitely small... a three-dimensional, fractal structure in perfect octaves.'

'A long, long time ago, Dave, I saw the Texan comedian Bill Hicks. Something he said really stuck in my mind. Something like this: "We are one consciousness experiencing itself subjectively. There is no such thing as death. Life is just a dream. We are the imagination of ourselves."

'That's pretty much the case, John. You see the laws, forces, and constants of the universe are fine-tuned for life, implying intelligence existed prior to matter. Space and time are not objects or things but rather tools of our animal understanding. We carry space and time around with us. The death of consciousness is simply not possible. Death only exists as a thought because people identify themselves with their body, believing that the body is going to perish sooner or later and thinking that consciousness will disappear too. If the body generates consciousness, then consciousness does die when the body dies. But if the body receives consciousness in the same way that a tuner receives satellite signals then of course consciousness does not end at the death of the physical vehicle. In fact, consciousness exists outside time and space. It's able to be anywhere in the human body and outside of it too. It's non-local in the same sense that quantum objects are non-local. End of sermon, John.'

Food for thought, but that was a while back. Now John found himself in a world of hurt and wondered who was creating it. What was the dream and who was the dreamer? Who was dreaming whom? Was Gevorkian's dream just more powerful than theirs? Could he overrule their reality? And what about Felix? The man obviously had their son in his power and was successfully manipulating him for his own ends - his desire for power and riches. If he could get hold of the algorithm he could ask the earth for it if it had the power to infiltrate the secret world of the Movement. Consortium versus Movement. The battle was on and they were caught up in it whether they liked it or not and John certainly didn't like it. As far as he was concerned the Movement was on a hiding to nothing. But then he didn't really know the nature of their game and just how they hoped to go about achieving their nefarious goals.

Chapter Ten
Nor Iron Bars a Cage
Life without God is like an unsharpened pencil - it has no point.

When Felix turned fourteen he started to behave very strangely. For several weeks he talked ceaselessly and hardly slept. Most of what he said was, to his parents, nonsense. There was his uncle March and his spell of manic depression and Susie, being a mathematical genius, was of course on the edge of madness herself! Felix's psychiatrist at the time of his abduction was Max Floyd. John went to see him while Susie worked on the shield and Biro made his way back to Cambridge.

John explained to Floyd what had happened to Felix without going into too much detail - just that he'd been kidnapped by Gevorkian, who he said was a business competitor out for revenge and some ransom cash.

Floyd put his head on one side, rubbed his chin and turned to John.

'Armenian did you say?'

'That's right.'

'Interesting.'

'Why?'

'Because a man called the office the other day, who said he had an emergency on his hands. He claimed he was looking after a young man who was ill. Said he was having delusions of grandeur. He asked what medication he should be given and told me he would pay for the information. I asked him for his name. He said he was called Ladislaw Pric.'

'You're kidding.'

'No, I'm not... but still... like Gevorkian he sounded Armenian or Russian, or some such.'

'My guess is Gevorkian told him to use that name to take the piss at his expense and yours too.' John mused on the fact that Gevorkian maybe did at least have a sense of humour.

'Yes, you're right there, John.'

'So what'd you tell Mr Prick?' John couldn't stifle a laugh and nor could Floyd but he quickly pulled himself together and tried to appear business-like.

'I told him that however much he offered me I couldn't suggest or prescribe any medication without meeting the patient and assessing him.' Floyd paused, scratching the side of his nose like doctors do.

'And?'

'He said I knew the young man.'

'I asked him how he knew and he hung up on me.'

'That was that?'

'That was that, John.'

And so the plot thickened. Ladislaw Pric indeed! It got to John, though, that if *they* thought that Felix needed medication things must be getting bad at that end. John worried about his son more and more and how he was coping as Jesus Christ or not as the case might be. He had to sit tight and wait for Susie to complete her work and for Biro to return to the fold, just hoping that Felix could hang in there.

He took a walk. He crossed King's Parade and went into the college. He stood looking out over the quad towards the chapel. It was deserted, quiet and starting to drizzle very gently. John went back over the parade to a classy menswear store and bought himself a big-brimmed black fedora and a trench-coat. Feeling like a Raymond Chandler hero he walked over to the chapel and entered. Immediately he was overwhelmed by its grandeur and beauty. Bach's Toccata and Fugue rolled out from the organ through the nave and up into the vaulted roof. It was awe inspiring. Gradually a warm confidence settled on him and he was swept away by the beauty of it all. The sun broke briefly through the rain-soaked clouds, sending shafts of rainbow light through the stained glass windows and across the walls. John had a strong feeling of déjà vu. It passed as quickly as it had arrived - just a fleeting shadow. He stood transfixed for several minutes then left the chapel and strolled down to the Cam deep in thought. He arrived at the river bank and watched the drizzle peppering the surface of the water. The light had faded further and a spiritual calm flowed in with the river. It was tranquil and it relaxed him. He felt his muscles loosen and soften. Two students strolled laughing along the opposite bank - a boy and a girl, holding hands. John could see the light of love in their eyes and he thought of Susie. He filled with a warm glow. There was so much to live for, so much to fight for and he saw that a fight was coming his way fast. John recalled a dedication that Ram Dass, the spiritual teacher, author of *Be Here Now* and friend of Timothy Leary, had written in a book he'd given him by Maharaj Charan Singh called *Spiritual Discourses*. It went something like this: "You can run but you can't hide. You can only grow into who you really are. You may think you're free to come and go and play where you will but the Beloved has taken you for his own, and in reality you can only surrender more and more to that divine attraction. Slowly but surely in a moment or over thousands of lifetimes, the Beloved reels you in until you merge back into the unitary state of Sat-Chit-Anand - the truth consciousness bliss of the Self."

John felt encouraged as he turned unwillingly away from the lovers and the river and made his way back towards the chapel. His comslink tinkled in his pocket. He took it out. It was Susie.

'How goes?'

'Done, John. We're ready to rock.'

'Well done, my love. I'll meet you at the office in ten. OK?'

'We'll be there.'

As John was crossing the parade he saw Comb-over come round the corner with another man. He waved at John to wait. The two men sidled up to him.

'Good day, John.'

'What can I do for you, Grimsthorne?'

'Just wanted to say hello and introduce you to my colleague here. He's just joined us from Aberdeen. John Smith, Detective Constable Drillbit.'

John rocked back on his heels doing everything he could to suppress a laugh. He managed a twisted smile.

'Delbert to you and me, John.'

John turned away. He felt somewhat hysterical. His head was spinning. It was maybe a reaction to all the stress and doubt - and that name! It was just too much right now.

John put out his hand. 'Pleased to meet you, Delbert.'

'Likewise.'

'So, what's happening, John?'

'Happening?'

'Yes.'

'With?'

Grimsthorne sighed. 'With Felix.'

'Ahh. Yes... well, under control I'd say.'

'Is he home then?'

'Not quite.'

'Not quite?'

'Nearly home. Probably tomorrow.'

'Really?'

'Yes, really.'

Throughout this exchange Drillbit had remained silent, just nodding sagely in response to Comb-over's words. He finally chipped in with, 'Don't you think we should get back to the station, sir?'

'Who pulled your chain, son?

Drillbit was taken aback but steadied himself. 'Sorry, Sir.'

'Should think so too.' Comb-over strode off with Drillbit in tow. He called over his shoulder to John. 'See you later, Mr Smith.'

'See you,' John said and thought. 'Not if I see you first.'

John walked quickly into the office, up the stairs and into reception. 'Biro back yet?'

'No but he's left Heathrow. Won't be long.'

'And Susie?'

'She's not here'.

'Any messages?'

'Charles Wells called about the China deal.'

'Which deal?

'Steel-Eyed Death.'

'Of course. Sorry, Mary. I'm a bit distracted right now what with Patrice's m...death and all.'

'Hopefully Biro can help you through.'

'Yes, he will. He always does.'

John went on into his office and sat down on the couch. He crossed his legs and straightened his back. He had to try and relax. He started to repeat his mantra. He thought of Swami Ji and things started to slow down. He went to the tranquil lake in his mind's eye. He saw the calm, motionless water. He saw the trees and the clouds. He saw the perfection. He heard the music and he touched something deep - a tranquillity beyond words. He had no idea how long he stayed there. It was a place outside time. He pulled back into the world when he heard Biro's familiar footsteps on the stairs. He came quietly into the room and sat down in a chair opposite John. He smiled gently and raised his hand in greeting.

Chapter Eleven
Steel-Eyed Death
When you meet a lion in the forest there's no need to worry.
The lion will know what to do.

'Hello again, John me boy.'

'Hi, Biro. Good to have you back.'

'When's Susie gonna be ready?'

'Any minute now.'

'I have a coupla my guys - very good, capable guys - waiting in the 'copter on the roof. They're setting up the tracking gear with Cakes. We could be good to go in ten minutes.'

They both turned to the door as Susie came in followed by Andy. She looked tired but as beautiful as ever. She was glowing with her achievement and held up a small black box towards John.

'That it?'

'Sure is, Biro.'

John stood, walked to Susie and looked deep into her brown, shining eyes. His left hand stroked her long blonde hair. His right took the box and turned it over in his hand. Susie's arm went round him and she pulled him close. He caught that wonderful, familiar scent of new-mown hay. He melted. Biro stood and took the box from his hand.

'We should go to the roof.' Biro moved to the door and looked back. John and Susie followed him out.

Baby Cakes and the boys were finishing up rigging the equipment as they stepped onto the roof. Susie and Andy prepared the shield locator/penetrator. Biro and John watched in silence. In fact nobody said anything much, engrossed in their work. With nothing to do John was just plain nervous. Susie nodded. John did the same. She took a remote from her pocket, put in some settings and with a smile in John's direction she pressed a button. They waited. Susie moved abruptly towards the 'copter.

'Let's go.'

They followed her and climbed aboard. As they sat and strapped in she spoke again. 'They're in a bunker in a field on the edge of a village called Fotheringhay in Northamptonshire. Near Oundle.'

'I know it. A friend of mine went to Oundle. Used to go over to visit him and we played squash in Fotheringhay.'

'Small world.'

'Sure is, Biro.'

'How far?' asked Andy.

''Bout thirty five miles. Should take us ten minutes in this.

Maybe less.'

Biro worked on his comslink. The 'copter rose rapidly and nosed down for the north. Susie broke the silence. 'If Gevorkian and his men aren't asleep they'll know we've located them and they'll wonder if we have the tech to penetrate the shield. They might just be packing up as fast as they can.'

'I've got some high speed drones coming in to cover all the exit roads.'

'Good thinking, Biro.

'I'd say we've got this thing covered.'

John nodded his agreement. Biro looked cool, calm and collected. John was quite the opposite. His knees were shaking and his mouth was so dry he could hardly swallow. He also felt stupid that he hadn't thought of the drones. Well, at least Biro had and drones were his department. He shrugged and felt a bit better.

The landscape sped by beneath them - a green blur. No one spoke for several minutes. John looked at Susie. He thought she must be thinking about Felix. He was wrong. She checked out the readers on the box and shook her head.

'What's up, Susie?'

'The penetrator won't lock in.'

'Big problem?'

'Looks like it, John. Should've kicked in by now. We're close enough.'

'Maybe not. Wait 'til we're on the ground.'

She looked very concerned and glanced down at the box again.

'We'll get him out, Susie.' John did his best to sound optimistic and strong.

'We will.' Biro glanced down at his comslink. 'The drones are over the village. No sign of a car or aircraft moving. Very quiet.'

'Too quiet.' John attempted a joke which, unsurprisingly, fell completely flat.

Biro announced loud and clear, 'Landfall one minute. Get ready for a rapid descent and be ready to jump.'

'Then what?' John asked.

'Follow me and do as I say.'

'OK, Bro'. You're the soldier.'

'Was.'

'Yeah but you know what's what.'

'Get ready.' Biro smacked his hands together and turned to the door. He was all power and focus.

John was overwhelmed with terror as he stood shakily. He

felt physically sick. Biro jumped with Baby-Cakes and his two boys followed in quick succession. Then Susie and John. Biro was already jogging across the field with a screen in his hand when they cleared the 'copter. He halted abruptly. An area of the meadow ahead of him was rising up to form a gentle mound with a diameter of about 10 metres. Susie and John stopped dead. They watched the turf roll back as doors in the dome started to open like a petal and then recede. Gevorkian's head, then his shoulders appeared in the centre of the opening. The lift came to rest and Gevorkian took one step towards them and stopped. The seven of them stood facing him off and waited. From the corner of John's eye he could see Susie. She was concentrated. She looked so beautiful in the golden rays of the setting sun. He was enchanted. She glanced at him, nodded and John came back down to earth.

Gevorkian held up his hand. 'That's as far as you can go.'

John stepped forward. 'OK but we found you. The net is closing in on you, Gevorkian.'

Gevorkian laughed. 'Like I said, that's as far as you can go.'

'For now.'

'For now?'

'Consider this: we have found you, so…'

'So what, John?'

'So we could maybe penetrate your shield.'

He thought for a few seconds then replied, 'I doubt it.'

'You can doubt it but you can't be sure.' John glanced at Susie. She shook her head. Gevorkian understood that they wouldn't break in today.

'We'll leave here soon and we'll take Felix with us unless you deliver the algorithm.'

'Not done yet.'

'Get on with it.'

This man was making John angry but he held himself in check.

'Remember this. If you use it before you hand it over we will know, I can assure you.'

Susie could not contain herself. 'How is Felix?'

'He's well - at least physically. We look after his bodily needs. But mentally...'

'Yes?'

'Mentally he's out to lunch.'

'Meaning?'

'Meaning, Professor, that he thinks he's Jesus Christ. Should I say, *knows* he is Jesus Christ. He has no doubts about *that*.'

Andy rocked back on his heels, wondering if he'd heard

right.

Susie hung her head. She was dejected. John walked over to her. They turned their backs on Gevorkian and looked at Biro. He nodded. Susie walked off. 'Let's go.'

They followed her.

'No good talking to anyone about this.'

They all stopped and turned back to the Armenian. John felt defiant. 'We don't intend talking to anyone. We don't need to. We can deal with *you*, Gevorkian, *ourselves*.'

He laughed. 'I doubt that…very much.'

They headed back to the 'copter.

'Can he really know if the algorithm has been used?'

'Yes, John, he can.'

'How?'

'It's not easy to explain.'

'Try me, Susie.'

'Remember the scalar weapon software that Gevorkian had hidden on your PC?'

'Of course. I'm hardly likely to forget that high point in my life.'

Biro laughed.

'I met you and Biro - best girl, best man. I have him to thank for that.'

'Love you, John.'

'I guess we must've known deep down that he'd be smart enough to be on top of that. So, tell us how he'll do it, Susie.'

'OK. I'll have a go. My guess is that Gevorkian would have gotten a really good grasp on scalar technology by now. So this is the essence and this is how he'd know if we'd used the algorithm. It's like this: a scalar wave can travel backward in time from the future to arrive at its source. When an electron jiggles it sends out radiating waves into both the past and the future. The future wave would hit a future particle, which would also wiggle, sending out its own advanced and retarded waves. The two sets of waves from these two electrons would cancel out except in the region between them. The zero point field of electromagnetic waves has its own substructure. The secondary field caused by the motion of subatomic particles interacting with this field are the scalar waves. They're not electromagnetic and they don't have direction or spin. These waves can travel far faster than light. Scalar waves encode the information of space and time into a timeless, spaceless quantum shorthand of interference patterns. This bottom-rung level of the zero point field - the mother of all fields - gives us the ultimate holographic blueprint of the world for all time – past and future.'

'Fuck!' exclaimed Biro. 'I could just follow you but I don't claim to understand what it all means... practically.'

'Very few people do, so you're not alone.'

'That's encouraging.' He glanced at John.

He shrugged and smiled, 'That's my girl!'

The 'copter landed on the roof of their office. They sat in silence for a while.

'I guess the question is this: can you get the penetrator to go? More precisely how long will it take you?'

Susie glanced at Andy. 'How long?'

'Dunno. Can't say... exactly.'

'Roughly.'

'Six to eight hours.'

'OK. Let's get started.'

John walked to the door. 'Biro and I'll wait here. The 'copter can take you two back to the lab. Keep us informed... please.'

'Sure will.'

Biro and John climbed out of the 'copter and it lifted off. Susie blew John a kiss and he did the same for her. As the aircraft pulled silently away John reflected on the translation of the Vaimanika Shastra written by Bharadvajy the Wise in fourth century BC. According to this ancient Indian text, the people had flying machines which were called Vimanas. The epic describes a Vimana as a double-deck, circular aircraft with portholes and a dome like a flying saucer. The text said that a Vimana flew with the 'speed of the wind' producing a 'melodious sound.' There were at least four different types of Vimanas. Some were saucer-shaped, some were long cylinders. They could switch the drive to solar energy from a free energy source which sounded to John like an anti-gravity drive. Adolph Hitler was intensely interested in ancient India and Tibet and sent expeditions to the region every year. This effort started in the early 1930s. The goal was to gather information on the Vimana flying machines. The 'copters, fixed-wing planes, ships and cars they rode were powered by electricity extracted from the earth's magnetic field, which gave them an inexhaustible supply of energy. And it was free.

Biro and John took the lift down to their Cambridge office.

Chapter Twelve
I Am What I Am

The death of the body is most often accompanied by less suffering than the death of the ego.

Felix sat up on his narrow bed in the salt cave and put on a bedside lamp. He glanced around. He looked puzzled as if he had no idea where he was. There is a book on the table beside him. It is *The Essene Gospel of John.* He stood slowly and walked across the salt covered floor into the bathroom. He peed, then looked hard at himself in the wall mirror and appeared surprised by what he saw. He touched the mirror, putting his palm flat on its surface, obscuring his face. He heard the door into the cave open as he stepped out of the bathroom.

Tigran Gevorkian was standing by the door, which he closed and locked. 'Good morning, my Lord.'

'Good morning, John.'

'What time is it?'

'4:30 am.'

'You're very early. To what do I owe this pleasure?'

Gevorkian shrugged and studied Felix in silence then said, 'Today.'

'Today what?'

'Today we are leaving here.'

'Why?'

'Circumstances dictate.' Gevorkian waited again. 'Aren't you pleased to be going out into the world?'

'Of course...and I'm ready.'

'Good. We leave at 8:30 tonight.' Gevorkian turned to leave.

'Before you go, I have two questions.'

'Go ahead.'

'I find it intriguing that you and my father have the same first name, as does the author of the book you loaned me.' Felix pointed at the book on his bedside table. 'Is this significant?'

'I don't think it is, my Lord.'

'Don't you?'

'No I don't. You often read significance into things that aren't significant.'

'Do I?'

'Yes, you do.'

'Are you sure about that?'

'Yes.'

'You should be cautious about rejecting the things I tell you. Remember John, I am what I am.'

'OK. Point taken. I'll leave you to your book now. I'll send someone to collect you when it's time to fly the coop.'

Tigran left the cave, locking the door behind him. Felix went to his table, sat down on the bed, opened the book and read out loud: '*And you, answered Jesus, be true sons of God, that you also may partake in His power and in the knowledge of all secrets. For wisdom and power can come only from the love of God. Love, therefore, your Heavenly Father and your Earthly Mother with all your heart and with all your spirit. And serve them that their angels may serve you also. Let all your deeds be sacrificed to God. And feed not Satan for the wage of sin is death. But with God lies the reward of the good, his love, which is knowledge and power of eternal life.*'

Felix stood and paced the salt floor with the book in his hand. He looked pained and started to cry. He fell to his knees, raised his hands open wide high above his head and said, 'Moses commanded your forefathers: Thou shalt not kill. But their hearts were hardened and they killed. Moses desired that at least they should not kill men, and he suffered them to kill beasts. And then the heart of your forefathers was hardened yet more, and they killed men and beasts likewise. But I do say to you: Kill neither men, nor beasts, nor yet the food which goes into your mouth. For life comes only from life, and from death comes always death. For everything which kills your foods, kills your bodies also. And everything which kills your bodies kills your souls. And your bodies become what your foods are even as your spirits likewise become what your thoughts are.' He bowed his head and lowered his hands to his side. He held his shoulders straight and his head high.

Upstairs Gevorkian and Seaweed watched Felix kneeling in silence. It was clear that what Gevorkian had seen and heard had made an impression on him. Though what that impression meant was not obvious. Seaweed looked nothing more or less than confused. Gevorkian closed the comslink and sat back in his chair. He nodded at Seaweed signaling that he should leave but just before he reached the door Gevorkian called him back. 'The 'copter must be primed for lift-off by o-six hundred, OK?'

'Yes, Boss.'

'And are all the men armed and ready?'

'Yes, they are, boss.'

'Good. And they know that they only open fire if we are trapped and have to fight our way out?'

'I've made that clear, boss.'

'We just have to hope that Susie Bellavista gives us the algorithm before tonight if we're going to leave here cool and calm.'

'Now laughing friends deride 'Tears I cannot hide…' Tigran nodded at Seaweed.

'So I smile and say…' Seaweed threw it back to Gevorkian.

'When a lovely flame dies smoke gets in your eyes.' He lapsed into silence, then, 'Thank you, Seaweed. I'm going to rest now.'

An hour later Felix was lying on his bed, staring at the ceiling. He sat up abruptly, stood and started to pace distractedly around the cave. He walked in erratic shrinking circles and stopped. He smacked the side of his head with a flat hand and then shook it violently as if trying to clear it.

'John! John! Come to me *now*!' He shouted. He soon heard a movement outside the door and a muffled voice. He waited. He felt footfalls on the stairs and Gevorkian came into the cave. His hands were behind his back.

'What is it, my Lord?'

'I am Merlin.'

'Merlin?'

'Yes, Merlin, the greatest shaman ever in the British Isles.' He waited for a response. None was forthcoming. 'He is a magician who has travelled the worlds within. He has known the astral plane and beyond. The truth has been revealed to him.'

'And the truth is?'

'The truth is that the one and only permanent thing in all the universe of universes is consciousness. Everything is consciousness. Absolutely everything. On *this* planet human beings are the only life-forms with enough awareness to be able to ask the question, "What is consciousness?"' Felix watched Gevorkian to see if he understood what he was being told. The Armenian nodded.

'Copters have no consciousness. Trees have some self-awareness and the animals - dogs in particular - have some small glimmer of self-consciousness but we humans have it full-on. We are aware of our own existence. We know that we are in this universe even if we don't know why.' Felix waited.

Gevorkian waited.

Felix continued, 'Space and time are the creations of the mind. The physical observable universe is an illusion. Time does not exist. It doesn't pass. We don't travel through it. It is always *now* - the eternal now. We can see the future just as we see the past if our consciousness rises up. We are consciousness - nothing more or nothing less. Get it?' Felix lapsed into silence and looked away from Gevorkian then said slowly and clearly, 'Bring me Amanita Muscaria.'

Gevorkian thought about this. 'D'you mean Fly Agaric, the basidiomycete fungus, my Lord?'

'I do indeed, Arthur. Yes.'

Slowly Gevorkian brought his hands from behind his back and held them out to Felix. In one hand he held out three boiled red-capped mushrooms. The damp and shiny surfaces of the caps were speckled with white dots. In the other hand he held a small, sharp knife.

We all know these mushrooms from illustrated books of fairy tales where very often Fly Agarics are a big feature of the scene. Felix did not bat an eyelid at the sight of the fungi but it made no sense. How could Gevorkian know about the mushrooms and where to get them? How did he know that Merlin would ask for them before the shaman actually did? This threw a whole light - or shadow - on things. To Felix it was all as natural as falling off a log.

'Here.' He proffered the mushrooms to Felix. 'Cut them and eat. I will fetch you a glass of water.'

Felix took the offering and cut up the mushrooms into small strips with the knife. Gevorkian offered him the water. Felix threw a handful of strips into his mouth and took a deep drink. He repeated the process until he had swallowed all the mushrooms.

'Lie down, my Lord, and relax. I will return to you later.' Gevorkian left the cave. Felix watched him go then lay down on his bed.

Seaweed was watching the cave monitor screen when Gevorkian came into the room and sat down next to him. 'How did you… happen… to have those mushrooms with you, boss? I couldn't believe what I was seeing.'

'You saw what you saw, Seaweed.' Gevorkian laughed. 'It was just one of those things. Just one of those crazy things.'

'A trip to the moon on gossamer wings.'

'Just one of those things.'

Both men laughed'

'I've had those mushrooms for a few weeks now. I had 'em couriered in from Siberia. That's where the most powerful ones grow and where they're easy enough to find. I read up about them and I thought they might be useful when the time to leave comes around. Felix will be disorientated once he has vomited and the mushrooms do their work. It was pure coincidence that I had them with me when he announced that he was Merlin. Matter of fact I was thinking of trying them out myself.' They laughed long and hard.

The thing, is dear reader, it is the Fly Agaric that has shown me the future. As Felix has just told us, there's no such thing as time. It's a continuum. Fly Agaric opens the door into that continuum. I travelled into the future beyond the events in this narrative so that I was able to look back from the future to the recent past.

Aspects of modern physics, such as the hypothetical tachyon particle and certain time-independent aspects of quantum mechanics, may allow particles or information to travel backward in time. My guess is that's how I knew exactly what had happened.

Chapter Thirteen
In The Beginning

In the beginning was the Word, and the Word was with God,
and the Word was God.
The Gospel According to St. John. Chapter One. Verse One.

Felix was lying flat out on his bed breathing gently when the Fly Agaric started to work its magic. He entered inside himself and found that he was in an unpleasant, murky underworld. He was stumbling through a region of muddy tangled roots. Mythical monster beasts appeared out of the gloom and quickly faded away. The stench of rotting bodies and decay was appalling. It sought to consume him but Felix wasn't frightened. A cheerful little ditty kept going round and round in his mind:

When I was young

I had a face like a clown

I stumbled around

Sighing my song

There was a continuous deep, ringing clang. It was unsettling. He slid on through the roots and the clanging changed slowly into perfect and utterly melodic music. The ditty faded from his mind to be replaced by St John Chapter One, Verse One. And he spoke it out loud, 'In the beginning was the Word, and the Word was with God, and Word was

God.' He knew instantly that the music was the sound of God, the word of God. This was it.

All thought ceased as a bright shining light came into his sight in the gloom. He felt himself propelled into the brightness. It was a portal into a verdant valley surrounded by majestic, soaring, white topped mountain peaks. Birds like tiny rainbows flitted through the trees and meadow grasses. The leaves glowed with a ringing radiance which echoed away into infinity. This was it. This was the thing in itself by itself. It was a world without end. It was boundless.

He heard horses' hooves in the grasses and four knights in intricately worked, glinting armour appeared. Their hair flowed out behind them in showers of light. The manes of the horses rippled and their tails created waves of colour. The horses drew up just short of Felix. The four knights dismounted and fell to their knees. One of them raised his head and looked hard at Felix. 'We are your guides across this region and up to the next plane.' His voice rang like bells and cascading waterfalls.

Felix bowed and the four knights turned their horses and led them off across the meadows. Felix followed, keeping close. The exquisite music was everywhere and in everything. His feet flowed across the grass on streams of glittering sound. Animals grazed all around harmoniously. A small angelic dog joined Felix and trotted along beside him. Felix looked down and smiled. Waves of love rippled through the dog from the top of its head to the tip of its swishing tail.

The ground rose up gently in front of them and they entered the next region. Felix, the dog, the knights and their horses became one joyful soaring song.

Eventually Felix came back into his body in the salt cave. He was himself. He was whole, balanced and cleansed. He had returned. The mania had passed and faded completely away. Gevorkian's plan had completely misfired.

Chapter Fourteen
Amanita Muscaria
The Soma of the Vedas

Fly Agaric has been a symbol of yuletide happiness in Central Europe, Russia and Scandinavia for centuries. It is called *a red light shining bright in the winter darkness*. This accounts for the red robes worn by Santa Claus and in the legend that he entered houses by descending down the chimney, which is interpreted as the spinal cord. Might this also be the source of the red nosed reindeer? This writer wonders if it is so. Of course there can be no doubt that the cap of the Fly Agaric does without a doubt resemble the conk of the fabled Rudolph. Then there's the fairy on the top of the evergreen Christmas tree.

Ingesting the Sacred Mushroom has been compared to drinking a glass of two milks.

You gotta wonder what that's all about.

Chapter Fifteen
Susie

Science without religion is lame.
Religion without science is blind.
Albert Einstein

John adored Susie. Always had. She was the love of his life. In fact if push came to shove he would lay down his life for her a hundred times over without a second thought. The same went for Felix and Bella-Blue too of course.

John and Biro were sitting in the production office waiting.

'You look miles away, John. What you thinking 'bout?'

John clicked back into the room. 'You're right. I was away. I was thinking about how and when we met.'

'You mean when you were nosing around in that skip lookin' for your computer.'

'Yup, Biro. As I recall you were looking for discarded furniture. It was an odd way to meet.'

'Sure was.' He swept his hand around the room. 'Things've certainly changed for us. We've done well, John, even if we're in the shit right now.'

John nodded his agreement and went back to his memories. 'Then all that money was given to me...and then the 9mm.'

'The Sig-Sauer.'

'Good gun.' John sighed. 'And then I met Susie that same day. The day everything changed for me. What a day!'

'What a day, John.'

'And at the end of it all when that cop arrived with the present from Comb-over - the beautiful Jane.' John looked sad.

'Thing is, John, most dogs don't live as long as fourteen. She was a good age.'

'I've said this before Biro but I'll say it again, Jane was an angel in a dog suit.'

'She was. Indeed she was. She lived in a happy family and she reflected that.'

'But she gave us plenty too.'

'There's no denying that.'

John looked wistful.

'Cheer up, my friend. We'll get through this... together. Always have. Won't be no different now.'

They looked at each other and smiled their brotherly smile.

'OK, Biro. You're right. We *can* do it.'

Biro laughed.

Susie and Andy were bent over a work bench with the penetrator in pieces in front of them when there was a knock on the lab door.

'See who is it Andy and if they wanna come in, stall 'em while I clear some of this away.'

Andy called out, 'Coming. Just hold on a minute.' He walked slowly and opened the door cautiously to be greeted by the head of the Department of Applied Mathematics, Serge Garrickson. 'Sir...can I help you?' Andy stepped back to allow Garrickson to enter.

Susie had draped a black cloth over the dismembered machine. Andy breathed a sigh of relief.

Garrickson was surprised to see Susie. 'What brings you, the theorist, to this den of iniquity, Professor Bellavista?'

'I had a practical issue to discuss with Andy - Dr Macadam.'

'D'you have a problem?'

'No sir, not really a problem. I just had an idea to set up a practical experiment related to my work.'

'You should've come to see me first, Professor, before you borrow my staff.'

'I know, sir, but it was no more than a tentative meeting to see if...'

Garrickson walked over to the bench, lifted the corner of the cloth and was about to look under it when Andy blurted out, 'Please don't lift that, sir. We have an experiment running where we can't let the components be exposed to light.'

Garrickson fingered the corner of the cloth.

'Please, sir… if you don't mind… I… er…'

'Take it easy, Dr Macadam. I know when I'm not wanted,' He laughed and left the room. Andy and Susie waited for the door to close. 'That was a close shave, Andy.'

'It certainly was, Prof. Wouldn't have gone well at all.'

'And could've blown our operation wide open and God knows what else! Let's get back to work.' Susie lifted the cloth and her eye was caught by the small white piece of paper under the corner. 'What's this?' She picked it up and read it out. 'Grimsthorne says be careful.' She was taken aback and looked up at Andy.

'What's that mean?'

'I don't know… exactly. Or as Quentin Tarantino would have asked, *What the fuckin' fuck is going on here?'*

Andy had to laugh. Professor Bellavista never ceased to amaze him. 'Who's Grimsthorne?'

'He's a cop.'

'A cop! Shit! He rocked back on his heels. 'I don't like the sound of this, Prof. I don't like it at all. Too many people seem to know what we're doing.'

'*Seem* to… yes… but, stay calm, Andy. Nothing's happened yet.'

'Yeh, OK but…'

'Let's just get on with this and get outa here soon's we can.' Susie was very concerned but she didn't show it. Apart from being an inspired mathematical genius, she was a courageous woman and a loving, dedicated mother. Felix's plight hung heavily on her. His bipolar condition was a considerable burden for Susie and John and his kidnapping was almost more than she could bear. She knew she had to be strong and face the facts. She knew too that they had to face up to Gevorkian and fight it out with him if they were going to bring off Felix's rescue. She wondered what kind of mental state her son would be in and whether he would come quietly if he still believed that he was Jesus Christ and that Gevorkian was John the Baptist.

Chapter Sixteen
Inside Felix

I don't know why we are here but I'm pretty sure it's not to enjoy ourselves.
Ludwig Wittgenstein

Felix thought long and hard while he waited for Gevorkian to collect him for the break-out. He had enough insight to realise that the manic episode was over but he dreaded the low that might, and probably would, follow on its heels. Right now he felt OK.

He picked up his copy of *The Essene Gospel of John*. He opened the book and flicked through seeking some inspiration. He read:

'O thou holy Angel of Water!

To that one dost thou give both splendour and glory

With health and with vigour of the body.

To him dost thou give a long, enduring life

And the Heavenly Sea, thereafter.

We worship all the holy waters

Which do quench the thirst of the earth,

All the holy waters that the Creator hath made,

And all the plants which the Creator hath made,

All of which are holy.'

He closed the book. He was uninspired. He thought about his mother and father and he worried for them and wondered how they were coping - if they were coping. He knew they would be desperately worried and unable to find him - or so he thought. He stood and paced the room. He was uneasy. Felix knew it wouldn't be long before Gevorkian came for him and they would be leaving. He felt a flutter in the pit of his stomach and his pulse began to race. He felt guilty and very sorry for himself.

He pondered his mental ups and downs. His parents had taken him to a psychiatrist, who had diagnosed that he had Bipolar Affective Disorder. This meant nothing to him but his parents understood the meaning of the diagnosis even if they didn't know what had caused Felix to contract the condition. After the consultation and when Felix had returned to school John and Susie discussed the diagnosis in depth. Their first reaction was that, given that Susie's Uncle March had been bipolar, it could well be genetic and that maybe it was something he had inherited even though there was no evidence they knew of that the condition could be transmitted in this way. The other possibility was that it was caused by some childhood trauma. They were not aware of any deep traumas in Felix's life but couldn't discount this possibility.

What they were not aware of was that Felix had smoked skunk on many occasions. He had come under pressure from his peers and had resisted for some time given that he knew it was illegal and could be dangerous. He had hidden his skunk smoking from his parents but if John and Susie had known they would have realised what had caused him to get ill.

Felix had not made the connection and was in denial that this could have caused his mood swings. His parents had told him about his great-uncle March's Klossowski's history of mental illness and to Felix this sounded like the most likely explanation. He was keen to smoke the drug again and get stoned. In a sense he was addicted if not physically then mentally. He didn't look into the condition so it had not occurred to him that there might be a link. He didn't feel comfortable reading about the illness. He didn't want to know.

But it began to dawn on Felix that he should continue to *appear* manic to Gevorkian and not let on that the episode was over. That way he could sensibly plot a way to escape from the clutches of the Armenian and his henchmen. Felix guessed they'd be armed when they made their break. A wave of fear washed through him. He did his best to calm himself and try to think clearly. He pinned his hopes on his athleticism and his success as a sprinter. He had won many cups at school and was rarely beaten in short-distance races. He had played right wing in the half-backs and there were few boys who could stop him once he had the ball. He could swerve, duck and weave and outrun the opposition. He hoped that this skill would give him the edge when he made his break - if he made his break.

Chapter Seventeen
Semper Fidelis

We are on the verge of another revolution in our understanding of the universe.
Arthur C. Clarke

Susie looked up to Andy from her work station. Triumph was written all over her face. Andy smiled and gave her a thumbs-up.

'I got it, Andy. Let's get outa of here.'

They threw off their white coats and headed for the door. Susie heard footsteps approaching. She moved her hand over a lighting console, plunging the room into darkness. They moved silently into a corner of the lab and waited, hardly daring to breath. They were so close to winning now. She resolved that nothing would stop them even if they had to fight their way out with their bare hands. In the event the footsteps passed on by and up the corridor. They moved back to the door and left the lab, ran down the stairs almost tripping over each other and burst out into the open. They leapt into the hover-car and Susie accelerated the vehicle into the air, heading fast for the roof of John's office. She called him 'We're on our way, Johnny boy. Get everyone aboard the 'copter and be ready to leave soon as we land.'

'Roger that, Susie. We're ready to rock!'

Half a minute later the hover-car set down on the roof. Susie climbed out, ran to John and held him tight. Biro hustled them onto the 'copter. It lifted off as soon as they were aboard and headed out at high speed towards Fotheringhay. Contrary to John's request Biro and his men all carried 9mm Sig-Sauer P226 automatics as he was sure they would need them and if push came to shove they would use them. They had all trained with the weapon and were crack shots, so there was next to no chance of hitting Felix - or so they firmly believed.

The 'copter flew low and fast out of Cambridge, heading for Huntingdon, which they passed on their right, and then pushed on for Oundle, making another right for Fotheringhay.

Susie broke the silence. 'Serge Garrickson visited us in Andy's lab.'

'Who's he?'

'Head of the Department of Applied Mathematics.'

'So?'

'So he nearly uncovered what we were doing and he left a note.'

'Please get to the point, Susie.'

'It said, *Grimsthorne says be careful*.'

'Grimsthorne! What's going on? Is the head of the

department his errand boy?"

'Dunno, John. Very strange.'

'What's the point of going to all that trouble?'

'Relax, John. You know the cop is on our side.'

'Do I, Biro?'

'I trust him.'

'And I find it hard to trust anyone.'

'Anyone?'

'Present company excepted, Susie.'

'Of course.'

John opened his comslink. 'Grimsthorne?... It's me, John Smith. Why'd you get Serge Garrickson to deliver your message to Susie?... He works for you... with you... what?... I don't get it... Well, OK. Tell me more when I see you. You gotta realise and accept that it wasn't exactly reassuring for Susie - and Andy... It was disturbing. Seemed like she was being watched from all sides... All right, all right I forgive you.'

Susie nodded at John. Biro shrugged. They set down close to the mound. Susie and Andy set to work with the penetrator.

At the same time Gevorkian's three henchmen wheeled their hover-copter onto the lift. He and Seaweed put handcuffs on Felix and blindfolded him then, as they stepped onto the platform, Gevorkian briefed his men. 'We may find we encounter some opposition. I'll put the boy aboard and while I wind up the 'copter I want you to set up flanking positions left and right so's you can set up a cross-fire enfilade and cut them down if they rush me. Break out the Uzis while we head up to the surface. I'll take down the shield if the coast is clear.'

'Got that, Boss.' Seaweed nodded to the other men.

One of them stepped forward, 'What's gonna happen to us, Boss?'

Gevorkian turned on him and snapped, 'Silence!'

The man stepped back in line. Seaweed snarled.

Gevorkian activated the lift. 'Here we go.' They started their ascent. The men were armed and ready, looking forward to some action. Gevorkian sang, 'A cigarette that bears a lipstick's traces…'

Seaweed picked it up. 'An airline tickets to romantic places.'

'And still my heart has wings. These foolish things remind me of you.' He stopped the lift before it cleared the shaft.

John and Susie's 'copter landed just as the lift had started up. Susie and Andy jumped from the aircraft and activated the penetrator. It came alive and the shield collapsed with a sharp, piercing crack. They knew they were in and so did Gevorkian. He checked around his men to see that they were all ready, that Felix's hands were cuffed and that his blindfold was tied tight. He had a plan.

'As soon as we're out in the open move real quick to your flanking positions. I will keep the boy close to me.' The dome doors opened. They could see the blue sky above them as they rose quickly to the surface.

John, Susie, Biro, Baby Cakes and his boys watched the dome open and the top of the 'copter start to come into view.

'OK, boys, spread out fast and be alert.' Biro pulled out his Sig and armed it. His men followed suit. John and Susie were surprised and dismayed by the automatics but quickly realised they were doing the right thing given Gevorkian's violent and ruthless history. Before they could get very far the 'copter came clear into view. They could see the four men run to left and right, their Uzis at the ready. They saw that Gevorkian was holding Felix tight at his side and that he was handcuffed and blindfolded. John and Susie looked at each other in dismay and then back to Felix. They felt helpless even though their team was armed. They knew they were outgunned. Good as the Sigs were, they were no match for the rapid-fire Uzis. John glanced at Biro. He looked cool and confident. He'd been under fire and outgunned before. He took the situation in his stride. 'One up the spout, boys. Hold your ground and your fire until I give the signal.' Each man cocked his weapon and gave Biro a thumbs-up.

Gevorkian stepped forward and shouted out. 'I am going to fly now with your son in the 'copter. Do not attempt to stop us. Do not attempt to follow us. If you do try my men will gun you down. They will then return to the bunker. I stress again, do not try to stop them. They can unleash more rounds in five seconds than you can in thirty. So if you want to live follow my instructions to the letter. Is that clear?'

John, Susie and Biro nodded their assent then watched in silence as Gevorkian steered Felix onto the aircraft, closed the doors and lifted off. They were gone in seconds into the wide blue yonder.

Chapter Eighteen
Hope Springs Eternal

O thou the last fulfilment of life, death, my death, come and whisper to me.
Rabindranath Tagore in Gitanjali

John, Susie, Biro and Baby Cakes watched the 'copter disappear then walked dejectedly with the other men back to their aircraft wondering what they could do to track the Armenian down. The prospect looked bleak and almost hopeless. They all felt ashamed to have failed poor Felix. Little did they know that the boy was more on the case than they realised. It was ironic that Gevorkian's attempt to disorientate Felix with the Fly Agaric had backfired. As it happened it broke him right out of his mania and left him clear. He was managing to fool Gevorkian, successfully maintaining his manic front.

Gevorkian flew the 'copter low and fast, heading for Formentera where he owned a magnificent and well-fortified seashore villa. Felix was still blindfolded and cuffed but he kept his cool, occasionally muttering nonsense to himself to maintain the image. He did what he thought Gevorkian would expect a manic to do.

Back at the office they did what they could to track the flight of Gevorkian's 'copter, calling everyone they knew in air traffic control but to no avail. Things looked hopeless again and all their efforts - particularly Susie's - had come to nothing. The poor girl was despondent. John did his best to comfort her even though he felt utterly lost himself.

'How 'bout a game of pool, John? Get your mind off things while we wait for one of us to have an idea.'

John thought about this offer. 'Thanks, Biro but not right now. Let's go for a walk, Susie.'

'Sure.'

They walked out onto King's Parade and into the college. They stopped and stood, overwhelmed by the grandeur and beauty of the chapel building. It never failed to impress when they stood up close to it even though they could see it all from John's office.

As they entered, the choir was processing through the chapel singing the Gregorian Chant *Deus in Adjutorium*. Gradually a warm confidence settled on John and Susie and they were swept up in the power of the service. The setting sun cast shafts of rainbow light through the stained glass windows, onto the walls and across the congregation. John took Susie's hand and managed a weak smile. They sat in silence, soaking up the mystical atmosphere.

Biro was playing poker with his men when John and Susie returned to the office. John walked up to the table. 'Five card stud?'

'S'right, John.'

'Judging by the pile of chips in front of you, Biro, you're well ahead.'

'S'right.' He looked carefully at John and Susie. 'You two look kinda calm.'

Susie sat down by the window. 'We went over to the chapel.'

'Any good?'

'Yes.'

'Even for non-Christians like your good selves.'

'Got nothing to do with Christianity.'

'How'd you mean, Susie?'

'It transcends that. It's transcendent. Just spiritual.'

They lapsed into silence. The game went on.

Chapter Nineteen
Keep On Rockin' In The Free World
We exist midway between the extremely large and the extremely small - between the universe at one end and the Planck Length at the other.

Sometime later the game finished and Biro had thoroughly cleaned up. They were having dinner at The Rainbow vegetarian restaurant two doors down from the office.

'So what we gonna do, Biro?'

'Somethin' did occur to me this afternoon.'

'What's that?'

'Well, Susie, it came back to me that Gevorkian has a big villa down on Formentera.'

'How'd you know?'

'When I was working for him as a roadie with one of the bands he managed, or rather screwed, he got totally smashed one night after a gig and was boasting about this and that - his Hispano Suiza and things. Talking of Spain and the car factory made him somewhat romantic and it loosened his tongue. Boasting again, he let slip that he had a house on Formentera. Could be that he's taken Felix there? There's a chance…'

'It's possible, I guess. What d'you think, John?'

'I think we should definitely go down there and have a

look round. We've nothing to lose. Better'n that just sitting about here tearing our hair out. Let's do it, Susie.'

'You're on.'

'First thing tomorrow?'

'Yes, Biro. First thing.'

Their main course arrived. Biro picked up his knife and fork. 'Strange thing is that during this debacle I've met a woman.'

'Met a woman? We all meet women.'

'You're winding me up, Susie.'

'Yeah, well, trying to.'

'I mean, you know, someone special.'

'I do declare the mighty Biro is blushing.'

'I am not.'

'You are too.'

John remained silent and downcast during this bantering. Biro glanced at him. 'Cheer up, John, my man. We're gonna get your boy back. Definitely we will. I know it.'

'How can you…?'

'Dunno how. Just feel a certainty deep down like I did when we launched our attack on Drumrunnie. We were outgunned then too and Gevorkian had the edge. He was safe in his castle with his heavily armed hoods and we were running around, duckin' and weavin' in the bushes. We won then and we'll do it again. We have the force on our side. Right, Susie?'

'Right, Biro.' They slapped a high five. 'Game on.'

'You bet, Susie. Game right on.'

'Sure but then we were only getting my computer back...'

'Only getting' your computer back! But Biro and I *and* Uncle March all put our lives on the line for you, John.'

Biro glanced at Susie. 'Yeah but I had an ulterior motive, Susie. I wanted my revenge on Tigran Gevorkian.'

Susie walked over to John and took him in her arms. She squeezed him tight then pulled away.

'It's a bit more serious this time, Susie. That bastard has *our son.*'

'And I have the algorithm. Remember. Bargaining power, John. We can do this without resorting to violence.'

'Still gonna take a coupla guns with us.'

'I guess.

'You guess right, John. Just like old times.'

John cracked a smile.

'Meet you at seven then.'

'G'night love birds. Sleep tight.'

Chapter Twenty
A Wondrous Place
In the quantum world the electron is neither a particle nor a wave.

By a simple and tragic twist of fate news reached Susie early next morning that her Uncle March had passed on. He had been rushed to Glasgow Royal Infirmary following a stroke but had died very soon after he'd been admitted.

Susie was first down for breakfast when the news was given to her by Mary. The timid girl found it very difficult to tell Susie but she managed to rise to the occasion. Susie was nibbling toast when John sat down opposite her. He could see that she was sad and suffering.

'What's the matter, darling? You look...'

Susie looked up at him and gathered her strength. 'Uncle March died yesterday. He had a stroke and...' She burst into tears.

John jumped to his feet and walked round the table, taking his wife in his arms. He held her and stroked her hair. 'That's so sad, Susie. He was a great man. I'll never forget him.' John lingered by Susie entrapped by her beauty.

Between her sobs Susie managed, 'Neither will I, John. He was family and more of a father to me than my natural own.'

'I know, I know. Bless him and bless you, Susie.'

'Thanks, John. 'Preciate it.'

Biro came into the dining room and took in the scene before him. 'What's up, you two?'

John stood up straight. There were tears in his eyes when he looked at Biro. 'March died yesterday.'

'Oh, dear me. I'm sorry to hear that, Susie. How very sad. The world will be a lesser place without that brave man.'

'I loved him a lot, Biro.'

'I know you did, Susie, and so did I.'

Susie stood up abruptly. 'I'll see you boys on the roof in ten minutes.' She turned and left the room. Biro watched John.

'Sure isn't a good start, John. D'you still wanna to carry on down to Formentera?'

'Must, Biro. Gotta try it.'

'Agreed, John. Let's get on and kick ass.'

'See you up there.'

'Sure. I'm ready to rock.'

'Me too, man.'

The three of them met on the roof by the 'copter five minutes later. Baby Cakes and the boys were already there, looking fearsome and powerful in their body armour and helmets.'

Biro strode towards the aircraft. 'OK, team, let's saddle up.'

They were quickly seated and the 'copter took off on auto-pilot heading fast for Hastings and the English Channel. They made good progress and were soon over the sparkling waters of the sea. The sun shone bright in a clear blue sky. Biro looked charged up and kept smiling at Baby Cakes. He was raring to get into the fight and was looking forward to some shooting action. John and Susie didn't look so positive or gung-ho. They held hands for comfort. John's mind was spinning. Susie tapped her pocket to make sure she still had the memory pad with the algorithm. She remained in shock from the news of March's death. It was going to take her a while to get over that. She had John and they had Bella-Blue safe and far away in Australia. They had avoided telling her anything of Felix's kidnapping. It would do no good worrying the girl all those miles away in the Land Down Under. Gevorkian had Felix. Right now they hadn't but by hook or by crook they would get him back. Susie smiled at Biro and he beamed back.

They made landfall just north of Abbeville and pushed on south. Susie went to the big fridge at the rear of the 'copter. She prepared a snack and brought the food round on trays along with glasses and bottles of spring water. As they got nearer to their destination the banter between Biro and his boys picked up speed and the quicker the miles seemed to tick away. Their confidence infected John and he warmed to their courage and enthusiasm for the job. In a strange way he started to look forward to the confrontation. His mind went back again to the firefight at Drumrunnie and the thrill he experienced then in company with March and Biro and with Susie waiting outside in the getaway car. He was proud with how he had overcome his fear, risen to the occasion and fired his weapon. The fact that he had not held the Sig with two hands as Biro had instructed him and his shot had ploughed into the ceiling, showering him with dust and plaster and that the flash of the discharge had rendered him temporarily half-blind and deafened was neither here nor there. Of course he could never have done it without Biro, his full support, his courage and his conviction. He was a true brother in arms. He glanced over at him and Biro gave him his big bold smile.

'Did I ever tell about my debacle with Edward Halfhead?' Biro asked.

Everyone laughed.

'No, it's true, god's honour. If you don't believe me you can go to St Paul's Church in Bedford and see his gravestone. A long time ago I was in a Special Forces unit guarding the big hangers at Cardington where they built airships like the ill-fated R101. There was some top secret development work goin' on and some of us had to go undercover to root out suspected terrorists who, it was thought, were attempting to sabotage the program. I was sent into Bedford to look around because I was known to have a good nose for trouble-makers. I hung out in the clubs and bars and quickly recognized the insurgents. I managed to worm my way into their confidence. I had been trained in this work and boy was I a good actor. 'Specially with my strong Eastern European accent, which I still had in spades in those far-off days. Anyway, I just wasn't good enough and I was exposed. I made a run for it. I was followed and there was one helluva fight out in the rail marshalling yards. Halfhead was just too confident and full of himself. He came after me alone. He got me in a corner and pulled his automatic on me. Big mistake. The upshot was I fired first, hit him above his right eyebrow and blew him away. He dropped like a stone. I ran for it and made it back to base unscathed. His death was reported in the local and national papers. Yes, we still had newspapers in those days. Turned out his name was Halfhead and he'd certainly lived up to it!'

Just then the 'copter was rocked and buffeted by heavy turbulence and Biro immediately took manual control, flying deftly through the roaring wind. They were coming up on the coast just south of Montpelier. A violent gust almost flipped the aircraft right over.

'We'd better put this bird down and quickly. Can't fight these forces and it's nigh on impossible for me to hold her in the air.' He wrestled to keep the aircraft steady and began to feel that their numbers were *all* coming up this time. Then he clicked. 'I remember a small airfield just outa Narbonne. I can see it coming up on the nav. Let's get down there. Strap in tighter and hold on. It might be a very rough set down.' Biro swung the craft in a wide arc and rushed her down towards the ground. She swung from left to right, up and down but with arms that felt like bursting, he held her steady and made a half decent landing. He shut down and turned to the others behind him. They all looked battered, crumpled and pale. 'I have a friend called Dave Rudley lives in Figueras. It's near here and he's a good guy. We go back a long way. Served together and saw some heavy combat back in the day.' He turned to the control console. 'I'll bell him. Who knows he might *even* be pleased to hear from me! While the team climbed out of the 'copter Biro waited.

'Hi, Dave? How're things?'... We're on our way to Formentera to sort out some delicate... business... can me and six friends stay the night at your place? We could go to a hotel but it'd be a lot more fun to catch up with you, old buddy. ...Cool. We'll pick up an auto and be with you in an hour... Thanks, man.'

Biro joined the others, who were sheltering in a small hanger. 'Dave'll put us up but before we go we gotta push the 'copter in here lest it blows right over or away. Susie, could you rustle up a hire auto to get over here in half an hour?'

'Yup. Will do. But where are we?'

'We're on the western edge of the airfield known locally as Krapp's Dust.'

'Krapp's Dust?'

'Yeh, well Susie, a guy called Krapp got dusted here by a stray element of the freewheelin' Sixth Panzer Division back in World War Two. Year was 1940. Krapp was trying hold back the German advance single handedly and got greased by a tank shell right over there. See that stone?'

Susie looked where Biro was pointing.

'That's where he was when the shell hit, blowing him into very tiny pieces. The resistance came through the next day and saw the bloody little bits and the stock of his rifle. They'd heard the gunfire and the familiar report of his weapon and pieced together what must have happened. And that, my dear

Susie, is how the place got its name.'

'Thank you. I feel for that Krapp guy, facing up and dying all alone.'

'It is impressive, Susie.'

She got on the line and ordered an auto to meet them. They pushed and shoved the 'copter into the small hanger. It was a tight fit and difficult to move in the screaming wind. Once it was safe inside they waited for the auto. It arrived three minutes later and they all climbed aboard. Biro programmed their destination and the auto sped off. The further south they moved the more the wind dropped and when they arrived at Dave Rudley's it had calmed right down. Dave had manufactured his house himself using a large scale array of 3D printers. It was modeled on Han Solo's Millenium Falcon. In fact it was an exact replica down to the finest detail and looked for all the world like it was about to fly. As they drew up a port opened with a hiss and a ramp projected onto the ground. Dave walked out and stood at the top of the ramp. He was wearing a perfect copy of the costume Harrison Ford wore as Han Solo in *Star Wars*.

As they climbed out of the auto Baby Cakes was the first to speak. 'Fuck me. Where are we?' He answered his own question. 'Mos Eisley!'

'You will never find a more wretched hive of scum and villainy', John added remembering Obi-Wan Kenobi's comment.

Dave walked over to them. 'Hi, folks. Welcome to the Millennium Falcon.'

He shook everyone's hand as Biro introduced his friends. 'Pleased to meet you all. Fancy making the jump to light speed?'

They laughed.

'Looks good, doesn't it?'

They concurred.

'Wait 'til you see inside.'

He turned and led them up the ramp. They were all vaguely familiar with parts of the interior of the Falcon from watching *Star Wars* many times. Big fans. But they were gobsmacked. The craft was perfect in every detail. Dave watched them, enjoying their reactions.

'You'll all have your own cabins. Got a lovely double for John and Susie.' He looked at Susie admiringly. She blushed.

'You're a very lucky man, John.'

'I know Dave. Not only does she look like a movie star but she's a maths genius too!'

'Please, John.'

'But it's true, Susie. You're one in a million and I'm one blessed idiot.'

'You're no idiot, John. Just an idiotic artist.'

'Is there a difference?'

'Course there is.

Dave led them onto the flight deck with all its blinking lights and screens.

'My god, Dave! This is so... cool.'

'And thank you, Biro. Fact is I'm very proud of it. Took me years to make.'

'Bet it did.

'You can sit at the controls if you want to.'

There was a rush for the pilot's chair and a fair amount of pushing and shoving.

'Hey, come on. Ladies first.'

'Thank you, Dave.' Susie sat and John stood behind like Chewbacca, looking over her shoulder.'

'I'd like to move in with you.'

Dave laughed. 'Sure, Biro, any time. But now, tell me what you're up to?'

'Going down to Formentera.'

'And why you going down there?'

'Pretty island.' Name comes from the Latin word

frumentarium.'

'Frumentarium?'

'Means granary. It was very fruitful in Roman times. 'Tisn't now, of course. Not verdant but still beautiful.'

'Sure. And...?'

'It's a very long story, Dave.'

'I got the time. Don't do much round here 'cept build spaceships.'

'OK. You remember that hood I told you about, Tigran Gevorkian.'

''Course I do. The Hispano Suiza's sweet revenge.'

'And John's computer.'

'The hidden file thing.'

'That's right.'

'So?'

'Gevorkian kidnapped John and Susie's son Felix and we think he maybe holed up in his villa on Formentera.'

'You think?'

'Yup. Just a hunch.'

'Your hunches are usually good, Biro.'

'Well, let us hope.'

'Why'd he kidnapped Felix?'

'Revenge and to get his car back.'

'Is that it?'

'No. That's not all.'

Dave glanced at Susie.

'Thing is. Felix is bipolar and he was ill - manic- when he was taken. He let slip that he'd heard me on the phone talking about an algorithm I was working on to get into the files of the New World Order.'

'You can do *that*?'

'Yeah. Can now.'

'Then Gevorkian announced that he would trade Felix for the algorithm.'

'But can't you use it before you trade?'

'Not so simple. They'd know if we had.'

'How?'

'It'd show.'

'Don't understand how but I'll take your word for it.'

'You should, Dave. Susie knows.'

'Take your word on that, Biro.'

'Best you do, old buddy.'

'So what's your plan?'

'Nuthin' too ostentatious.'

'You mean like you're just gonna knock on the door and ask to trade.'

'We can't let him have the algorithm, Dave. It's too important given the scale of the threat that the world faces from the Order.'

'Don't know much 'bout that, Susie.'

'Time you did, Dave. So let me tell you something about it. The goal of the movement is global domination and the creation of a one-world government with a one-world currency and a one-world police force – all under the control of the international bankers. A very small percentage of the population estimated to be 'bout 5000 want to create and control an all-white world. So what the movement fears most are truth and the human spirit getting out of their control.'

'Fuck!'

'Just so.'

Biro picked up the story. 'So what we gonna have to do, Dave, is take the place by storm.'

'Sounds like you might be needin' the help of Han Solo. Got space for another soldier?'

'Guess we could squeeze you in, Dave.'

'When we going?'

'Soon's we can.'

'First thing tomorrow.'

'Let's do it, John.'

Next morning they retrieved the 'copter and flew along the coast as far as Toroella de Montgri then headed out over the sea towards Palma. Jock came through on the comslink.

'You there, John?'

'Yup.'

'Good news for you.'

'Makes a change.'

'Those two assassins were Russian. The search team has tracked them down. They're Secret Service with a touch of Mafia. Their real names are Konstantin Irinski and Fyodor Tolstoy. There are no apparent links to your Tigran Gevorkian.'

'Mine!'

'Well, you know what I mean.'

'Thanks, Jock.'

John turned to Biro. 'Don't seem the names are gonna be much help.'

'Somethin' to squeeze out of Gevorkian.'

'They flew on in silence for a few miles.'

'Where's the villa, Biro?'

'Out on the Mola.'

'So what's your plan?'

'Haven't got one yet, John. Suggest we over fly at altitude

and hack in with mag-scope. Do a survey and let the infrared tell us how many bodies are on site. Should give us the complete picture.'

Chapter Twenty One
The Billion Dollar Bash
The dew drop slips into the shining sea
Just as the sea slips into the drop...

Felix was holding cool, playing the part of the manic messiah and he was enjoying it. He had a strong feeling that help was close and rapidly getting closer. Intuition. It never failed him. Well, not often.

He stood on the terrace overlooking a high-walled courtyard which was filled with trees and bright beds of flowers under sprinklers. Two armed guards in very dark sunglasses, carrying Uzis and open com-links patrolled the walls. Felix had not seen Gevorkian all day though Seaweed had been up to his luxurious apartment twice to check on him. Felix had continued his charade as Merlin, the chosen one and only son of God. Seaweed had been satisfied that all was well and went each time to report as much to his boss. Gevorkian had ordered another batch of Siberian Fly Agaric and it had been delivered by courier that morning. He boiled up the mushrooms, took them down to Felix and offered them to him. Felix ate them immediately without a second thought.

Gevorkian suspected that Biro might recall his Formentera hideaway and sooner or later make his way there. Of course he had no idea just how close they were - at that very moment they were high in the sky above him.

The 'copter hovered silently while Biro, John and Susie studied the image on the big monitor screen. They could see Felix on his balcony. Susie's heart skipped and John held her hand. Biro pointed to the two armed guards. There was no one else in sight but in infrared mode they could see two other bodies inside the villa.

'So 'part from Felix there are four of them. One being presumably, Gevorkian. So not much opposition considering there are six of us.'

'Ever the optimist.'

'That's me, John.'

'Yeah but there's a high wall round the site and probably lots of guns inside.'

'Sure, but we have surprise on our side. They don't know we're here. Gevorkian may have figured out that I'd think of this but he doesn't know for sure. Must make him nervous, don't you think?'

'I do.'

'Thanks, Susie.'

'Where d'you think we should put down, Biro?'

'I know the island like the back of my hand. Came with

Gevorkian years ago and stayed for three months. So I'd say, Cap de Barbaria. I know a spot - a dip in the land - where the 'copter can get in and be hidden. There's a ruined farm house with some of its roof where we can sleep. Not many people go out to the Cap. Most locals and visitors stay in the villages or in beach accommodation.'

'How long will it take to get from the Cap to his villa?'

'It's 'bout sixteen klicks. Should take us under twenty minutes to drive or just a coupla minutes if we fly in.'

On the terrace in the bright sunlight under a clear, blue sky Felix started his inner journey once more and made it quickly through the dark region, rapidly moving to the light. He was met again by the four knights and the dog and then proceeded up the rise into the next region. A word formed within what was Felix and it was '*thus*'. This was the thus-ness of it all. The entity known as Felix dissolved into the one consciousness that is the universe of all universes. The infinite love. The eternal now: without beginning, without end. All and everything. At all times and in all places it was the now. Shape and colour merged into one glorious flaming light in music from nowhere and from everywhere. It was not born and it could never die. It was what it was - a network of pearls, so arranged that if one was seen all the others were reflected in it.

The spirit of the eternal Mother appeared and bestowed her blessings. In his being-ness there were words. *In every particle of dust there are present Buddhas without number.* Felix, the consciousness, flowed on in the endless river of light and sound. It was the bliss that is what it is.

I am the creation from the beginning. Everything in the creation is
me.

All creation is growing towards me.

It is begun in ecstasy.

It is continued in ecstasy

It is sustained in ecstasy.

It will end in ecstasy.

As the sun appeared on the horizon and blazed across the water in waves of shimmering light Felix returned into his ego body refreshed and renewed in wisdom.

Meanwhile, over on the Cap, the rescuers breakfasted and readied themselves for the task that lay ahead. There was little conversation as they steeled themselves for action. Biro opened his backpack and rummaged around inside. He pulled out two deep black 9mm Sig-Sauers and handed one to John.

'Just like the old days, John. And let's play it like that. We'll overfly the villa again first. If the two goons are in the courtyard we'll land on the roof, go into the building, locate

Gevorkian, grab him then search out Felix and get outa there. If there's no one in the courtyard we're fucked...no, seriously...we'll do the same thing. Get in there as quick as we can and shoot our way through to Gevorkian and Felix. Just like at Drumrunnie you stay in the 'copter, Susie, and be ready to fly off fast as soon as we're all aboard. OK? Any questions?' Biro looked around the group. They all nodded their agreement and understanding.

Biro, Dave and Baby Cakes went outside and pulled the tarp covering clear of the 'copter. They walked around the aircraft checking it over. Satisfied that it was in good order they went back into the farmhouse.

'Sun's nearly up. Let's get ready to rock and kick some o' that arse into the wide blue yonder.' Biro pulled on a flak jacket and zipped it. The others followed suit. He sat in the pilot's seat then cranked up the power. 'Burning and churning. Let's go.'

John looked pale. Susie was calm and collected. Baby Cakes and the boys were hot to trot, clutching their Sigs tight to their chests. The 'copter lifted off and, tilting her nose down, she surged forward into the morning. They climbed fast and were soon over the villa. Biro kicked in the infrared scope. The two guards were already patrolling the walls, Uzis in their hands.

'Looks good. The goons are in the courtyard.' He looked back at the team and gave them a thumbs up. 'Let's do it!' The 'copter descended fast and silently, settling on the roof with a gentle whistle of pneumatics. The 'copter door slid open. 'Out! Follow me.' Susie slid into the pilot's seat.

The first person they saw was Felix. He ran to John. 'Dad! I knew you'd do it.' They hugged.

'Get in the 'copter Felix. Mum's there.'

Felix dashed to the aircraft whooping with joy as he climbed aboard.

Biro led the team off the roof at speed. They spread out, going through the rooms. Baby Cakes found Gevorkian and laughed. The Armenian swung round and his jaw dropped.

'Hands up, mother-fucker, and don't move from that spot.' Biro and John joined them. They bound the dejected Gevorkian's wrists tight behind his back and led him from the room. Downstairs Biro's boys opened fire on the guards as they hurtled into the house. They aimed high but they pinned them down, disarmed and tied them up. The goons hadn't the courage to stand up to the boys. Just wanted to live and see another sunrise. No more shots were fired that day.

Susie clasped Felix tight to her. 'I'm OK, Mum. I knew you and Dad 'd save me.'

'Thank you. But I *am* your mother.'

'And you're really somethin'.'

'Sweet of you to say that but I'm just an ordinary gal.'

'Ordinary! You're much more than that, Mum. Apart from being a beautiful maths genius, you're the best a boy could hope for. And where would Dad be without you?'

'Your Dad 'd be OK. He has that true creative spark and he has drive and faith too.'

'I know, Mum, and I love him.'

Felix saw his father and the others appear on the roof. 'I must tell you that Gevorkian gave me some Fly Agaric. I took it and went on an amazing trip and when it was over the mania had passed and I was *myself* again.'

'Fly Agaric!'

'I ate some more mushrooms yesterday and went on another and even more amazing journey. Tell you all about it sometime.'

Biro and Baby Cakes hauled Gevorkian aboard and threw him into a corner. Dave and the two boys joined them. Susie turned to check that everyone was in and the 'copter lifted off, heading north across the gleaming sea.

Biro glances back at Gevorkian. 'Will you look at that, folks? We have him. The great Armenian gangster brought to heel. It's over for you, my man. And d'you know what you remind me of Tigran?' He waited. Gevorkian stared down at the space between his feet. 'You're just like the fabled Ouzelum Bird.'

'Ouzelum Bird?'

'S'right, John. When that bird is startled it flies round in ever-decreasing circles until it disappears up its own arse hole!'

'That so?'

'Sure is, Susie. 'Course that trick makes the bird something of a rarity.'

Chapter Twenty Two
One Step Forward
*For the successful accomplishment of any work one needs a
sharp intellect and the will to perform relentless Karma.'*
Rig Veda

Back home again John, Susie, Felix and Biro discussed the future - particularly what to do with and about Gevorkian. He was currently under lock and key in the basement of the King's Parade office. Baby Cakes and the boys kept a twenty four hour watch. They knew how smart and crafty he was. When he was taken food two men went in and one stood outside. He complained about his exclusively vegetarian diet. He wanted steak. He wanted pig. He wanted dead animals. Baby Cakes was disgusted and told him in no uncertain terms to, 'shut the fuck up!' and to eat what he was given and be grateful for it. As far as Baby Cakes was concerned the world would be a much better place without Tigran Gevorkian.

'Let's let him stew down there a few days. Soften him up somewhat. I have an idea which I'd like to put to you when I've applied the algorithm and got inside the Movement's site.'

'OK, Susie, when you gonna do that?'

'Tonight, John.'

Susie went into her office and fired up her ethernet

connections. She ran the algorithm and watched it stream like lightning through the complex array of firewalls, false leads and dead ends like a knife through butter and right to the core. She glowed as she gloried in the power of her vision and mathematical prowess. It was not her ego that felt this but something wider, bigger and close to divine.

She saved what she'd found, fully encrypted it and hid it on their local system. She backed out slowly from the Movement's site and systems, covering her tracks like a burglar or a murderer might wipe his prints off everything - absolutely everything - he had touched or on which he might somehow have left traces of his DNA. Susie knew she was good and that they could never follow her trail in or out. She was quite simply so much smarter than they were.

Susie was horrified and very badly shaken. She found the facts she'd uncovered almost beyond belief. She had discovered that the Movement's scientists had successfully managed to create a powerful and unstoppable, genetically modified virus that would attack and kill all the non-white peoples of the world using a tested and selective DNA pattern reader. The virus had been built on the Nano scale using a synthetically created rotary molecular motor made up from a three-bladed triptycene rotor and a helicene capable of performing a unidirectional 120° rotation. The system consisted of a bis-helicene connected by an alkene double bond displaying axial chirality and having two stereocentres. This was the key and Susie understood it, even if no one else on the team did!

Released into the air the virus would complete its grisly task in a mere forty eight hours, leaving the desired all white-skinned world and a whole lot of clearing up.

She discussed what she'd found with John, Biro and Felix late into the night. The facts were terrifying and way too awful to get a hold of. They were all in shock and they knew that the Movement must be stopped dead in its tracks before they could put their insane plans into action.

'So here's my idea. Think carefully about it before you dismiss it out of hand.'

'OK, Susie. Let's have it.' John leaned back in his chair to listen.

'We let Gevorkian go…'

'What!'

'Let me finish, please, Biro.'

'We let him go free to infiltrate the Movement but with a quantum state tracker implant in his skull so that to all intents and purposes we'll be literally in his head!'

'Wow.'

'We can also program the tracker to auto-destruct at any time, taking the wearer with it.'

'Wicked... and cool!'

'Yes, Biro, it is, as you rightly observe, cool. So we'll instruct Gevorkian to ingratiate himself with the Movement and win their confidence. Given what we know, we can tell him certain things about them, which'll impress them into revealing more about their plans and lead Gevorkian into the holy of holies. His job may be to kill all the members of the central committee. I hope not. He'll then return to us and we'll pay him off. Perhaps you should consider sacrificing the Hispano Suiza to the cause.'

'No way.'

'Think about it, Biro. He'll be a wanted man. They'll track him down and eliminate him. We'll know where your beloved car is and we can go right ahead and get it back for you. The movement won't want it. It's too hot.'

'It is that, Susie.'

'So, my boys, what do you think?'

Felix was the first to speak. 'But is it...ethical, Mum?'

'You mean like thou shalt not kill?'

'Exactly.'

'Well, Felix, let me remind you that the Movement plan to eliminate all the races which are not white with that virus. So I say yes it is ethical.'

'Me too, Susie.'

'Thanks, John. Biro?'

'Yup, I say grease the mother-fuckers - all of 'em.'

'Succinctly put, Biro, and in your own inimitable style.'

'Well, thank you, ma'am.'

'My pleasure, kind sir.'

'You see, Felix, it boils down to sacrificing a few to save the many.'

'OK, Mum. I get it and I'm with you all the way…and back.'

'Thank you.'

Chapter Twenty Three
The New World Order

Sometimes you have to do the thing you least want to do even when you know that people who don't deserve it will be hurt.
Dominic Bryant in the film *Nothing and Everywhere*

They brought an angry and confused Gevorkian up from the basement and into the office. They were all there: John, Susie, Felix, Biro and Baby Cakes. Gevorkian glared at Felix, who smiled back brightly.

John pointed to a chair. 'Sit down, Gevorkian.'

'I...'

'Shut the fuck up and listen.'

Gevorkian shrugged, trying to look cool and commanding.

John stood and walked over to stand in front of the Armenian. 'This is how it is for you now. We're in charge and *you* will do as you're told. Understood?'

Gevorkian shrugged again.

'We're going to implant a micro sensor at the base of your brain.'

Biro added, 'If you have one.'

Gevorkian flipped. He went to lunge at Biro, who pushed him back hard into his chair.

'The sensor will track your every move and relay

everything you see and everything that you say and that's said to you. 'When the sensor is in place you will go to Salt Lake City where you will present yourself at the headquarters of the New World Order Movement. We are going to give you some information on the Movement, which will impress and scare the living shit out of 'em because the information is top secret and technically impossible to come by. If you're forced to you can tell them that you know what you know from a Russian Mafia boss. You will also tell them that you have no idea just how this information was collected. We expect that they'll welcome you with open arms in the hope that through you they can discover how the information was obtained. Clear so far?'

This time Gevorkian did not shrug but growled, 'Yes.'

'Good. 'If you step out of line we'll know and you will die. We require that you infiltrate to the very core of the organization and when you have their confidence you will kill each and every member of the central committee if you have to. If you succeed in this task - and you will - we will give you back the Hispano Suiza and a false identity. If you haven't already, we suggest you make a will.'

John paused. 'Now, what about Constantin Irinski and Fyodor Tolstoy?'

Gevorkian looked blank.

'Constantin Irinski and Fyodor Tolstoy. Russians.'

'What about them?'

'Do they work for you?'

Gevorkian threw back his head and roared with laughter. 'Me? No. They are KGB.'

'Are they after you?'

'After me?'

'Yes.'

'No. What is all this? Fuck you all.'

Biro stood over Gevorkian. 'Zip it!'

'So who sent them to Afghan to kill our stills photographer?'

'What!'

'Yes, that's what they did.' John waited for a response. 'Why?'

Gevorkian thought hard. 'Me and the KGB don't mix.'

'I assumed…'

'Could be to show they know.'

'Know what?'

'Know about me taking Felix.'

'Why'd that interest them?'

'Because Susie is Felix's mother.'

'So?'

'So they're KGB undercover operatives, who have most likely been spying on Susie and her department for many years.'

'Why?'

'Because they know that's where things start... science things, new ideas...'

'I still don't get it.' Nor did anyone else in the room.

'It's a way to catch me, John.'

'I thought you said they weren't after you.'

'That's true. Not me but what I can get for them.'

'What can you get for them?'

'Don't be obtuse, John. The algorithm.'

'But, how?'

'Through me, through Felix, through you, Susie.'

'So we have the KGB to contend with now!'

'No, you don't, John.'

'How's that?'

'They're no longer with us.'

'Meaning?'

'Meaning those two are dead.'

Biro was taken aback. 'What!' This was ruthless even by the Armenian's standards.

'How? When?'

'Seaweed took care of 'em a coupla days ago, John.'

'Seaweed?'

'My trusty sidekick, Susie.'

With that cleared up if in a somewhat muddy way, John shrugged. 'You will leave in two days. We'll start your briefing tonight. Baby Cakes.'

'Boss.'

'Take him back downstairs and watch him like a hawk. He's a slimy, evil bastard but he's sharp and smart.'

Baby Cakes called in his boys and they led Gevorkian out of the office and back down to the basement.

'I think he's got the picture.' Susie smiled. 'I gotta gut feeling we're gonna win this one.'

'Save the world?'

'Yes, Felix, I know it sounds just a tad grandiose but, as you say, save the world.'

Chapter Twenty Four
Go Forth Upon Thy Journey
Out from under the Wings of the Illuminati

They inserted the tracker and gave Gevorkian a first class return air ticket to Salt Lake City. They booked him a suite in the best hotel in the city. They wanted to keep him happy and create an imposing impression on the Movement. They arranged for him to have a deluxe auto and gave him a wodge of spending credits. They had inserted the tracker and briefed him the night before with plenty of juicy tempting goodies to be going on with. If he needed more stuff they could give it to him.

They flew Gevorkian out to Heathrow and waved him off with a cheery bye-bye. The Armenian looked decidedly pissed off. In fact, he was trying to cover his fear. For all his tough guy posturing he was a weak man, who knew he was caught in a trap largely of his own making and that he had no choice but to comply. But he felt his mood changing. Something in him relished the challenge ahead. All through his life he had fought to combat his insecurity by putting on a brave face, posing as a ruthless tough guy. Eventually he grew into this projection and lived out the life of a greedy, vicious thug, hell-bent on power - power for its own sake. He never questioned his motives, never went near his conscience. He had the rugged good looks of an Armenian peasant and that was exactly what he was. Low-born and ill-educated, living off his wits and on his ability to frighten others with his terrifying brand of hostility. He grew deep into this role and relished it.

Now Gevorkian was beginning to experience something new. He was feeling the first stirrings of empathy. He was doing something for others and not just for himself. It was a strange and unnerving sensation and one he had never been near before. For once in his life he felt he was part of something positive and worthwhile.

The HQ of the Movement was an anonymous grey, windowless tower. Gevorkian walked up to the building. The entrance was indicated by a small sign, which read simply NWO. A sweet female voice asked, 'Can I help you?'

Gevorkian spoke towards the sign. 'I would like to speak to Helen Simpson.'

'D'you have an appointment?'

'No.'

'I'm sorry but you'll have to make an appointment.'

'That's not good enough.'

'Can I ask, why?'

'No you can't, but you *can* tell her it's in relation to General Harold Gataxis and the Movement.'

'General Gataxis?'

'That's what I said.'

'I...'

'Speak to Helen Simpson *now* and tell her I have some important information regarding General Gataxis. Got that?'

'Yes, Sir. Please wait.'

Thirty seconds later. 'Please, come in. I'll send someone to meet you in reception immediately. What's your name, Sir?'

Gevorkian didn't respond.

'I'm sorry. I didn't catch that.'

'That's because I didn't say anything.'

The hidden door in front of him slid open silently and Gevorkian stepped into the building.

'Our boy's doing good.' John was with Susie, Felix and Biro in the Cambridge office with the comslink open.

'He is, Biro. Surprisingly good', John responded.'

'I'd say he's got the picture.'

'So'd I, Susie.'

John walked to the water fountain. 'Mentioning Gataxis like that really hit the spot.'

'I'd say he rang just the right bell.'

An elegant young woman walked out of the lift and approached Gevorkian. 'Would you please follow me, Sir.' She went back to the lift and Gevorkian followed her. The doors shut and they ascended silently. The girl nodded to Gevorkian to follow her. They walked down a long corridor with doors to left and right. One opened silently and they entered a spacious office with views over the city. A glamorous blonde stood to shake Gevorkian's hand.

'Mr...?'

'Gevorkian didn't respond. He stood silently and waited, his eyes fixed unblinking on Helen Simpson.

'Have a seat, please.'

Gevorkian accepted the offer and Simpson sat down opposite him. She didn't seem at all sure how to begin. 'General Gataxis...'

'Yes?'

'What d'you know about General Gataxis?'

'That information doesn't come cheap.'

'Err... what d'you want?'

'To talk to the Chairman.'

'He's a busy man.'

'I don't give a flying fuck how busy he is.'

Simpson flinched.

'Contact him. I will see him *now*.'

'He may not...'

'He will. Mention Gataxis *and* Senator Godfrey Peel. He'll see me.'

Simpson walked to her desk and depressed a pad. 'I have a gentleman here who would like to talk with you about General Gataxis and Senator Peel.'

A voice snapped back. 'Bring him up here immediately, Miss Simpson.'

Once more Gevorkian followed the woman into the lift. When they stepped out they walked directly into an enormous office, which was dominated by the biggest oak desk Gevorkian had ever seen. A man stood by the picture window with his back to Gevorkian.

'Mister is good enough for now. Who are you?'

'I am the Chairman.'

'I believe you but what's your name?'

'The Chairman.'

The man continued to stare out over the city. 'What d'you know about Gataxis and Peel?'

'I don't enjoy talking to a man with his back turned to me. It's very rude and I won't accept it.'

'I do not wish you to see my face.'

'Tough shit, Chairman. I won't answer you until I *can* see your face.'

The Chairman didn't turn.

'If that's your best shot I'm leaving and if anyone follows me I will kill them.'

The man turned and Gevorkian recognized him immediately. He was Aaron Lieberman, the CEO of the extreme right-wing news channel Wolf News.

'Ah, it's you. I might've guessed.'

'Sit down please.'

'That's better.' Gevorkian sat. He felt good. He had control. He knew he had the power.

'This guy's just amazing. We made the right move and we chose well.' Susie smiled triumphantly around the room.

'We sure did, darling.'

The Chairman spoke again, 'So tell me, sir, what d'you know about General Gataxis and Senator Peel?'

'You mean apart from the fact that one's a General and the other's a Senator?'

'Precisely.'

'I know about the part they'll be playing when you put your plans into action.'

All the Chairman's poise deserted him He was visibly shaken. 'How...?'

'If you think I'm gonna tell you how I know what I know you're right out of your tiny mother-fuckin' mind.'

The Chairman rocked back in his chair. 'There's no call for you to be offensive.'

'Ha! Offensive! That's a good one considering what you and your nasty friends have in mind.'

The Chairman took a deep breath doing his best to stay calm in the face of what he realized was a very serious threat to their security and plans. 'I... er...'

'Let *me* tell *you* this. We're onto you and we are going to blow your plans to kingdom come unless...'

'Unless what?'

'Unless I join you.'

'You want to join us?'

'You're getting the idea, Aaron.'

'I'll have to...'

'What?'

'Discuss this with my colleagues.'

'No, you don't have to, fuck face. You will inform them that I will be on the Central Committee as of now. Got it?'

'I...'

'Just do as you're told and all will be well.'

The Chairman nodded his assent.

'And let me tell you this, if you try to imprison me or harm me in any way *my* colleagues will know about it and it'll be curtains for you and The New World Order. Do I make myself absolutely clear?'

'Yes, you do.'

'Well get on it then.'

The Chairman didn't move.

'Right now!'

The Chairman jumped to his feet and ran like rabbit from a gun.

'He's brilliant. What a J-O-B!'

'Ain't he just, Biro?

John nodded his agreement. 'We're in there. Gevorkian's really come up trumps. What d'you think, Felix?'

'Always knew he was smart… and tough. Though regards the latter it was all a front. Seems like he might just have a heart of gold.'

'Don't know 'bout that.'

'Remember, Susie, he knows we're listening in and that if he steps out of line we can kill him.'

Biro clapped his hands. 'I love it.'

'I love it too, Biro.'

'Attaboy, Felix.'

Chapter Twenty Five
Don't fuck with me Argentina.
**Following the invasion of the Falkland Islands
and the sinking of the Light Cruiser, the Belgrano, Margaret
Thatcher was heard singing this in her bath.**

Tigran Gevorkian was lying on the bed in his hotel suite. He was communicating with Cambridge. He looked relaxed. John and Susie were sitting side by side on the big comslink screen.

'I'm on the committee and have complete free rein in the building. No one is permitted to approach me or question me. I go where I please. They're very frightened of me and what I might say or do, So how d'you want me to proceed?'

'First off, Tigran...'

'Ah, so it's Tigran now, Professor Bellavista.'

'I get the feeling that you are more engaged with our work than you might care to admit.'

'Don't have much choice, do I?'

'True. But you're making an ace job of it. You completely spooked the Chairman.'

'And enjoyed it,' added John.

'Yup, I'm enjoying it. I'm moving in a powerful circle. Makes me feel good to mix and match with the rich and powerful.' Gevorkian laughed.

'Rather you than me.'

'So what next?'

'Find out what you can about how they plan to release the virus and where.'

'Shouldn't be too difficult. No one follows me."

'Good.'

'Then what?'

'Then we want the full dope on the virus - the strain, the molecular structure, the gene run…that kind of thing.'

'That might not be so easy, Prof.'

'Ah, Prof is it now?' Susie laughed. 'You can do it, Tigran. Tell 'em you also know about Admiral Fortuna's involvement. That should really rattle their cage. According to their files he's a top player and his part in the plot is more masked than any other?'

'Why's that?'

'Dunno.'

'Maybe they plan to release the virus from low flying carrier-borne aircraft.'

'That would indeed make perfect sense, Felix.'

Biro agreed. 'Yes it would. In fact my guess is that's it.'

Chapter Twenty Six
A Dry Wank

The non-existent was not and the existent was not at that time. The atmosphere was not nor the heavens which are beyond. What was concealed? Where? In whose protection?
Rig Veda

Gevorkian followed the two men down a passage finished in a glowing white material. The guides were dressed in tight fitting, fully sealed white suits as was Gevorkian. All three wore helmets with no apertures. Air was fed into their helmets by micro compressors on their belts. Images from the observable universe were conveyed directly to their retinas through the ether band. Sounds were conveyed to their ear drums by the same method. They stopped outside a fortified door while their identities were checked and verified. A portal opened before them and they stepped through. Gevorkian wondered if Cambridge could see and hear what he was seeing and hearing. He sincerely hoped so.

They entered a large high-ceilinged laboratory manned by similarly attired technicians sitting at work stations and surrounded by banks of monitor screens and lab equipment. No one acknowledged their presence. One of the guides turned to Gevorkian.

'This is the main development area for the virus.' The man

then went into a deep and thorough explanation of how the virus was being developed, its molecular structure, how and why it would achieve the desired goals and how it would be launched on an unsuspecting and unprepared world. The virus will be stored in that secure vault over there.' The man pointed to a door at the end of the lab.

Gevorkian listened, amazed that he could extract such delicate intel so quickly and easily. But it was all gobbledygook to him. He just hoped that Cambridge was listening in and recording the presentation. There was absolutely no way that he would remember even a small fraction of what he was being told. Even though his suit was temperature controlled he was starting to sweat. His head was spinning. He wished that the presentation would finish and that he could get the hell out of the lab, indeed right out of the building. Hardcore gangster that he was, he was spooked and horrified by what was being planned. He was on board with Cambridge good and proper. He was a changing man and he felt the first faint flush of altruism. It was an entirely new experience for the Armenian and it was good.

The moment he was back in his hotel suite he was so freaked out that he attempted to masturbate but it didn't go anywhere. It was, as they say in the medical profession, a dry wank and Gevorkian gave up on the task. He kicked in the comslink to Cambridge. John and Susie were listening to a live broadcast from King's College of Gregorio Allegri's Miserere. It was a setting of Psalm 51. They were so taken up in the music that they ignored the flashing screen. They both knew the piece by heart. It was one of their favourites. In the section they were listening to the Italian libretto is translated as:

What a mystery my life is.

What a mystery!

I am a sinner from the year 80,000.

A liar!

But where am I?

What am I doing?

How do I live?

I live in the soul of the world -

Lost in the depths of life.

Eventually they dragged their attention away from the music and focused on the screen. In Salt Lake City Gevorkian was strumming his fingers impatiently and when he saw he had their attention he asked, 'Did you see it? Did you hear it?'

'We got it all, Tigran'

'Good.' Tigran sighed with relief. He had no wish to go through all that again. 'What next?'

'We have a meeting today with the Prime Minister and the heads of MI5, MI6 and the Secret Service.'

Tigran was impressed. 'You people don't hang about.'

'There's no time to hang about.'

'Guess not. What d'you want me to do?'

'Just keep your eyes and ears open and stay cool.'

'If I can.'

'You must.'

'I'll do my best.'

'I'm sure you will.' Susie paused. 'Oh, and by the way, you won't have to kill anyone.'

'Pity.'

'Yeh, well…we're gonna take a more subtle approach.'

'Way to go, Professor.'

Chapter Twenty Seven
A World Without End

The smile that you give out comes back to you.
Brian Wilson of the Beach Boys

John, Susie, Biro and Felix flew to London and set down on the roof of the HQ of MI6. They were ushered into a sound-proof room where they were introduced to the PM and the heads of the three departments. The Foreign and Home Secretaries were also there though they didn't say much.

Susie opened the meeting. 'Given that we now have all the intel we need on the virus and the delivery method, I suggest we set about creating and testing an antidote.'

'How long will this take?'

'Well, Prime Minister, if we have a big enough team and all the specialists we need we should be able to crack it in one week.'

'Is that fast enough?'

'It'll have to be.'

The head of MI6 asked, 'What about delivery?' How d'you plan to do that?'

'We're keeping that to ourselves. Still working on it.'

John glanced at Susie and wondered.

'One way or another we'll coerce 'em.'

'How?'

'Well, sir. We know much more about their A team membership than we've revealed to them or to you for that matter.'

'Are you going to inform us now?'

John stepped forward. 'Prepare yourselves for a shock.' He waited until he had their undivided attention. 'The US Secretary of State.'

'Mandy Hatherton!' The Prime Minister looked thoroughly unhinged. The other three department chiefs were rocked to their foundations.

'The very same, sir.'

'But…but that's impossible!'

'It may *seem* impossible to you but I can assure you all that it's the truth.'

Susie picked up the story. 'You're obviously aware that this lady is on the extreme right politically and that she's Christian fundamentalist.'

MI5 spoke for the first time, 'Well, yes fair enough but it's a big leap from right wing fundamentalist to being behind a plot to exterminate half the human race.'

'And more!'

'Yes, OK, and more.'

The Prime Minister pulled himself together. 'But she was here only last week and as sweet as pie.'

Biro laughed. 'Yup, well, like most politicians she's a good actress.'

The Prime Minister let that one go.

The Secret Service man spoke for the first time. 'We have a secure and secret bunker complex in Wales. We'll take you there as soon as you're ready. You will travel together in a windowless auto. All your comslinks will be disabled before you enter the complex.'

The Prime Minister stood. 'Good. Please let us have a full list of the equipment you'll be needing and job descriptions of the required staff.'

Susie took out a memory pod from the pocket of her jacket and held it out towards the Prime Minister. He nodded to MI5, who stood and took it from Susie. 'Thank you.'

The Prime Minister headed towards the door. 'When'll you be ready to leave for the facility?'

'As soon as you have everything in place. We'll work fast and be in touch.'

The heads of the departments followed the PM out of the room.

Chapter Twenty Eight
The Mist of Mystery

And I entered and beheld with the eye of my soul, above my mind, that light unchangeable.
Saint Augustine

During the flight back to Cambridge Biro asked the obvious question. 'I assume you'll manage to create the virus antidote but question is, how we gonna deliver it. Susie?'

'Just starting to get an idea.'

John turned to look at his wife. He was impressed. 'Trust, Susie', he thought. They lapsed into silence and waited.

Susie said nothing more until the team had assembled and were seated in the office.

'OK, boys, this is how we do it. Gevorkian has to hang in there and keep going. He must be reminded to never, ever drop his guard. I don't know how you feel but I think he's really getting off on it.'

John nodded his agreement.

And Biro quipped, 'For sure he is.'

Felix looked lost and somewhat out of his depth. He had very bad memories of Gevorkian and what he suffered at the hands of the Armenian. His palms were sweating and his mouth went dry just thinking about him.

'Now this is the part you're not gonna like. You'll agree that someone has to courier the antidote over the pond and into the Movement's HQ. Yes?'

They all nodded their agreement. John was starting to get a really bad feeling about what was coming next.

'Fact is, it's gotta be me.'

'Why?'

'Think about it, John. I'm a college professor with a senior ranking and I know more about computing and programming than all of you put together. Am I right?'

'You most definitely do, Susie.'

'Thank you, Biro.'

'Hey there. Don't include me in that sweeping statement please.'

'But it's true, John. 'Pared to Susie we've got shit for brains.'

'God help me!'

'Please stop it. Bickering will get us nowhere fast.'

'Hey. Got a really good joke that fits the occasion.'

'Go on then, Felix, lighten us up.'

'Thanks, Mum. There's this silent order of monks and they're allowed to speak once a year. So when the time comes around this one monk - let's call him Ivan - gets up at breakfast and says, "I want to complain about the lumpy porridge." He does the same thing, the next year and the next and this goes on for over a decade. Around about the twelfth year after Ivan has made his complaint another monk gets to his feet and passionately exclaims, "I am leaving the order. I can no longer tolerate this constant bickering about the lumpy porridge!'

'Very good, Felix. Very good.'

'Thanks, Dad.'

Susie sat down. 'OK, back to more urgent matters.'

'Don't be a spoil sport, Mum!'

'So I'm the courier. With my credentials I should sail through immigration. Remember too I'm a US citizen.'

'Fair point, Susie but if they stop you…'

'Thing is, John, I can hide it well. I'll wrap the phial, which'll be very small, in non-conductive organic material and then hide it.'

'Where?'

'Where'd you think, Biro?'

'Ah… yes. Well, I guess.'

John stood up abruptly. 'I'm coming with you, Susie.'

'No, John. We daren't risk both our lives. You have other responsibilities…' She glanced at Felix.'

'But, Mum… I…'

'No, Felix. Dad must stay here with you.'

Silence descended on the meeting. Susie broke it eventually. 'Gevorkian'll tell The Chairman that I know about The Secretary of State and others and that I'll let this news out into the world 'less they'll see me.'

'Will they buy that?'

'We've gotta hope so, Biro. It's our only chance - our last card.'

'OK, Mum but once you've got the meeting, what then?'

'Then I work on how to get into the virus vault.'

'Won't be easy.'

'What is, John?'

John shrugs and turns away.

'I can do it. I guess I'm smarter than them in any case and I can hack into anything I want however well it's protected. You all know that. Look, apart from being a very cool mathematician, I'm a wild frontier Kentucky gal. I'm part Cherokee remember. I'm hard core. I can protect myself and I know my way around.' She threw herself back in her chair, convulsed with laughter, then splutters out, 'Ain't no one better fuck wid me!'

Chapter Twenty Nine
The Great Mother

The Mother not only governs all from above
But she descends into this lesser triple universe.
She has consented to the great sacrifice
And has put on the forms of the ignorant like a mask.
Mother Meera.

And so the brilliant, wild and beautiful Cherokee Kentucky girl headed off to the US of fuckin' A with the phial tucked snugly between her legs. And John was left wishing he could be there too.

Once Susie had made landfall, passed through immigration and customs and reclaimed her luggage she walked out of the terminal. It had been a piece of piss but she kept her eyes open. She was intensely alert. She hired a deluxe auto and, once aboard, contacted Gevorkian. She instructed him to meet her immediately.

'90 miles north east of the city you'll find the Uinta-Wasatch-Cache National Park. Head for Haystack Mountain. When you get close you'll see an abandoned 70s style hotel called The Freaks Inn. I'll meet you in back by the ground floor kitchen. See you there at sixteen hundred. Make sure you're not followed.'

'I've got me a coupla minders. They can watch my back on

the way out.'

'Even though I'll have my hair tucked up under a trilby and wearing a Han Solo mask I don't want 'em in the building.'

'Indiana Jones meets Han Solo!'

'Precisely, Tigran.'

Susie went to her hotel room. She slipped the phial out of her vagina and put it in a hollowed-out copy of Melville's *Moby Dick* on her bedside table. She placed a half empty glass of water onto the book, punched in the *Do Not Disturb* display and left the room, taking her door card with her.

The drive out to the national park was pleasant enough but Susie was on edge. She felt overwhelmed by the task ahead and she was very afraid. She wanted John and Biro beside her but that wasn't going to happen and she knew it. All she had now to rely on and support her was Tigran Gevorkian and she wasn't convinced she could trust him further than she could throw him - and with her life too! But she wasn't spoilt for choice.

Susie parked the auto in a thick grove of trees and walked, masked and hatted, the last half klick to the deserted, crumbling ex-hotel, keeping her eyes and ears open. She saw Tigran approaching with two men on the other side of the building. Susie could tell that one of them was Tigran's sideman, Seaweed. They stopped and Tigran pointed to a small hillock to his left. They nodded to him and walked over to the mound, disappearing behind it. Tigran carried on to the hotel. Susie watched him enter the building and continued towards it herself. A small herd of deer scattered as she approached them and it startled her just as much as she had startled them. She pressed on and moved silently inside. She walked carefully through the debris strewn ground floor and entered the kitchen. Broken shutters creaked in the breeze and fragments of glass crunched under her feet. The place stank of rot and mould.

'Tigran, you there?'

'Over here, Professor.' He emerged from the shadows and approached Susie. They shook hands. They didn't bother with chit-chat or pleasantries.

'I have the anti-virus.'

Tigran nodded.

'Here's what we're gonna do. I'm going to hack the local system and download the key codes for the lab door and the virus vault. You will then use that code to get inside and put one drop of my magic mixture into each canister. If the canisters need a code to open them I will get that for you too.'

'How'm I gonna get into the vault without being seen or

triggering an alarm?'

'Hold on.' First thing is, I have to get into the building to hack their system.'

'Not easy, Prof.'

'I know that.'

'So, how?'

'You gonna tell them that the Prof who hacked their system knows about the Secretary of State and that if they don't see her she'll blow the whistle on 'em and that they'd better see her and be real quick about it.'

'And?'

'And once I'm in the building and meeting the Chairman I'll say I need to pee or words to that effect. He'll let me go because he'll want to know what I know. I will be the one calling the shots. I have all the aces in my hand and I play a mean game a' poker, Tigran.'

The Armenian was awestruck and impressed. He realised that Susie could do it and that she probably would. He was putty in her hands.

'Once I'm in the can I'll need only thirty seconds or so to get all the codes laid onto my micro reader then I'm outa there and back in the meeting and they won't know nothin' 'bout it.'

'Cool, Prof. I just hope for both our sakes that you're right 'bout this.'

'I am right, Tigran.'

'It's gonna be very dodgy for me breakin' into the vault and drippin' in the anti-virus.'

'Yeah but you can do it, Tigran. You're one tough, cool dude.'

'You're just too kind, Susie.'

'I know I am but it's true. It's good to have you on our team and callin' me Susie too.'

They shook hands and Susie drew him close. They hugged and he got that scent of new-mown hay.

'There is a God! See, Tigran?'

'Yes, I see and I've seen the light.'

'So, on we go, my friend.'

'On we go.'

'OK. Let 'em know I'll be coming and I'll go in there in the morning and demand to see the Chairman and lay it on him. When I've got the codes I'll meet you at the vault door then stand guard while you're in there.'

'And if you're disturbed, what then?'

'I have my methods, Tigran.'

'Which are?'

'I call them boobs. What d'you call them? Tits, I'd guess.'

Tigran blushes at Susie's frankness.

'Well, look at you, tough guy. You're blushing.'

He laughed and looked away. 'I don't call 'em anything' said Tigran with a smile.

'Don't'cha think it'll work?'

'It'd certainly work on me, Susie.'

'See what I mean? You're all the same, you men. Breast obsessed.'

'You are one cool girl.'

'Ain't I just, Tigran? See I know what I got and how to use it when I need to. I'm not just a pretty face, my Armenian friend.'

'John would love to hear you now.'

'Not too sure 'bout that.' She laughs her pretty, musical laugh.

'Drop-dead gorgeous', thought Tigran but he didn't say it. He had more sense.

Chapter Thirty
The Deep Bond of Love
The truth must dazzle gradually...or all the world will be blinded.
Emily Dickinson

It was midnight and the HQ was quiet.

'Please excuse me, Chairman. I have to use the rest room.' Susie stood and he did too and with an elaborate gentlemanly bow. Susie knew she had him. She left the office and walked down the corridor to the ladies' rest room. It was empty. She went into a cubicle and activated her micro reader. She tapped in some code and waited. In ten seconds she had everything she needed. It was far easier and faster than she'd expected.

Back in the Chairman's office Susie didn't sit down but stood facing him with her back to the window. He looked decidedly uneasy and right on his edge.

'So, Miss...Cartwright?'

'So we know that the Secretary of State, Mandy Hatherton is working with you.'

'Mandy Hatherton!'

'Yes.'

'Are you sure of that?'

'Yes, we are sure of that. We know it for a *fact*.'

'Er… who is this 'we'?'

'That's none of your business, Aaron.' Susie waited then walked purposefully to the desk and stood over him.'

'So… er… what do you want?'

'We'll come to that in due course. First I suggest that you consult with your colleagues.'

'I…?'

'Yes.'

'Do it then. Now. I'll meet you back here in fifteen minutes. Is that clear?'

Yes. Clear.'

'Well, look sharp and get on with it.'

Susie left the office, took the lift down to next floor and went into the rest room. She called up Tigran on an encrypted circuit. 'Meet me at the lab door in five minutes.'

'Roger that, Prof.'

As expected the lab area was deserted as she and Gevorkian reached the door at the same time. She scanned in the code from her reader and the door opened with an irritating hiss.

'em again. Got that?'

'Yes, Prof.'

'Go on then. Do it. If you work with clarity and conviction

it should take you no more than four minutes. I'll be right here when you return. Don't worry, Tigran, you can do it and I'll be watching your back.'

Tigran pulled on a pair of plastic gloves and went into lab. It was sufficiently lit for him to see his way. He followed Susie's instructions to the letter and rejoined her in just over three minutes. He looked pleased with himself.

'Done?'

'Yes, just as you instructed me. I took great care.'

'Well done. Let's get outa here.'

Susie went back to the Chairman's office. Gevorkian left the building and returned to their hotel. She was in the office and seated two minutes before the Chairman. He stood uneasily just inside the door.

'What is it you want, Miss Cartwright? You just have to ask... whatever it takes to buy your silence we'll...'

'My silence will not come cheap. I'm leaving now and I'll be back tomorrow or the day after to name my price.'

'But...?'

'Yes?'

'Can't we decide now?'

'No, we can't. I... we... want you to sweat it out and really feel the fear. We can blow this whole operation wide open any time we choose. Is that understood?'

'Yes, understood.'

'Goodbye. I'll be back.' Susie strode out of the office and cleared the building in two minutes.

The Chairman keyed a code. 'Launch the attack right now! No questions. Right now! I want the operation concluded within the next ten hours... good.'

Chapter Thirty One
Heaven's Door
Mama, put my guns in the ground
I can't shoot them anymore.
Bob Dylan

Mission accomplished. Four hours later Gevorkian and Susie were well on the way back to London. They sat in First Class. A bottle of the best champagne and two glasses sat on the table between them. They looked relaxed but Susie was concerned. She knew that the Chairman would have ordered a strike the moment she was out of his office. She calculated that the virus would be released by the time they were back in Cambridge if their shenanigans had not been discovered. She said a silent prayer and took a sip of champagne. She smiled at Gevorkian.

'You finish it Tigran. I'm going to sleep.'

'Thank you, Prof. Good night. Sleep well.'

Susie didn't wake until the rubber kissed the runway at Heathrow. They cleared immigration then customs and met John, Felix and Biro on the 'copter platform. Hugs all round. Tigran beamed and they took off for London.

'Given that the Chairman will have launched the strike as soon as I left him we can assume that in two hours or so we'll know if we've succeeded. If nothing happens and there are no deaths we'll contact the PM and they can blow the Movement wide open.'

'That's my girl!'

'I have to tell you, John. Susie was amazing. So brave, so smart. She scared the shit out of the Chairman from what she tells me and had him just about begging for mercy.'

'Oh, please, boys, that's enough. I'll tell you this, Tigran's a brave man too and he's clever. It was real good to have him as my partner.'

'That's true praise coming from you, Prof.'

'We were so worried about you, Mum. I don't think Dad slept a wink while you were away.'

'Not that you got much either, Felix. I think we both felt guilty that we'd let you go it alone.'

'But you understand why, don't you, John?'

'I do, yes. But we both felt we were missing out on all the fun and games too!'

The following day the US and UK governments combined came down on the Movement like a ton of bricks and the operation was shut down. The main players all ended up with long stretches in stir. Some of them got life, which they more than richly deserved, considering they planned genocide on an unheard of and unprecedented scale.

Biro got rid of the Sig-Sauers. One fine morning he and Felix buried them deep in the chalky soil of the Gog Magog Hills just south of Cambridge. They knew they would never need 'em again - not ever.

Chapter Thirty Two
A Glass of Two Milks
It is always better to put the needs of others before your own.

John, Susie, Biro, Felix and Tigran went out to dinner to celebrate. Well, they deserved it, didn't they? They *had* saved the world or at least a large part of it! A waitress came to their table to take a drinks order. Susie went for sparkling water. John and Biro asked for alcohol-free beers. Tigran ordered a double whisky. And Felix requested *'a glass of two milks'*. He flushed. It was the straw that broke the camel's back. They all but collapsed in a heap of heaving laughter. The attention of the other diners was attracted by the sound. With not much to see they all commenced to do what they were doing before their heads were turned. It was the wrong way to ask of course for two glasses of milk, but it seemed so very right to them all at the time.

Life, dear reader, went on much as before. And the Famous Five lived happily ever after. Possibly.

www.ingramcontent.com/pod-product-compliance
Lightning Source LLC
Chambersburg PA
CBHW060050260626
47160CB00005B/1642